Book

Narrow is the Way

Lowell Gridley

Lowell D. Gridley

Names, characters and incidents depicted in this book are products of the author's imagination or are used fictitiously. Any resemblance to actual events, locales, organizations, or persons, living or dead, is entirely coincidental and beyond the intent of the author or the publisher.

No part of this book may be reproduced or transmitted in any form or by any means, electronic or mechanical, including photocopying, recording or by any information storage and retrieval system, without permission in writing from the publisher.

ISBN: 978-1-933582-88-7

© 2014 Lowell Gridley

Cover Illustrations: **Savannah Ward**

Printed in the United States of America

Dedication

Thanks be to God that allowed or caused experiences in my own life from which to draw some of the ideas for this work of fiction.

Some <u>Narrow is the Way</u> characters

Ben Reed--forest ranger
Becky Reed--Ben's wife
Daniel----------------------------Ben's and Becky's first child
Steve, Sharon, and Grace--------------------the Serpa family
Mark, Melinda, Nick, Savannah-------Pastor McKenzie and family
Alvin and Alice Rush--------------ox cart owner and his wife
Sandy------------------------------Nick's friend and classmate
Jody--Sandy's mother
Randy --Sandy's father
Claude and Relda------------cattle truck owner, and his wife
Mr. Kirkland----------------------------------a school teacher

NARROW IS THE WAY

Narrow is the Way plan:
Character list

Prologue
Chap 1   Home Sweet Home
Chap 2   Due Date
Chap 3   Shaken
Chap 4   Called
Chap 5   Differences
Chap 6   Timber!
Chap 7   Comparing Beliefs
Chap 8   Coloring Books
Chap 9   Dry, Very Dry
Chap 10   Halloween? No
Chap 11   Wise Decisions/The Plan
Chap 12   Adult Drama
Chap 13   The Kids' Experiment
Chap 14   The Kids' Drama
Chap 15   The Performance
Chap 16   Movie
Chap 17   Ranger School
Chap 18   Seeking Wisdom
Chap 19   Oops/Explanations
Chap 20   Snow Rescue
Chap 21   Howard's New Bible
Chap 22   Nicodemus
Chap 23   Bruised and Deflated
Chap 24   A New Friend

Chap 25 Small Letters
Chap 26 Mine!
Chap 27 Private
Chap 28 Thank-you Visit
Chap 29 Let there be Lights
Chap 30 Who and Why?
Chap 31 Church Visitor
Chap 32 Whiteout
Chap 33 The KBC
Chap 34 Bearcats
Chap 35 Centennial

NARROW IS THE WAY

PROLOGUE

Over three years earlier, Ben Reed had gone with his friend Bob to have his first solo hang glider flight. Partially because of the camouflaged color of his glider, and also because the force of the sudden front wind they encountered, his crash landing site was not found. He had landed much farther into the mountains than anyone had searched. The search finally had to be called off. This left him in the mountains alone for two months. Ben started remembering a few things. What he recalled was enough to give him hope that there might be someone who knew him, and also knew where he lived. One of those things he seemed to remember was a number. Another was a name, Becky. The number turned out to be Becky's telephone number which he called when he had found a phone booth in a village at the foot of the mountains. At first Becky thought Ben's early morning call to her was a cruel prank; after all, how could he still be alive? She drove several hours to get Ben after she knew he really was alive. She had been his sweetheart before his accident.

Ben resumed his forest ranger duties. Eventually, the only thing he could not remember was his wild hang glider ride and subsequent crash. After secretly building a nice log house at the edge of the forest park, he asked Becky to marry him.

Steve and Sharon were two of Ben and Becky's friends. They lived on a ranch which they owned several miles south of the forest park that Ben was in charge of. Steve had been influenced by Ben to again seek the meaning of life while living it, instead of while trying to run away from it, which had taken place before his marriage. Sharon is still searching for the proper recipe to happiness. Becky is trying her best to help Sharon to do just that.

Claude, a cattle trucker, at times sought Ben's advice as he faced troubling situations. Ben in turn, had received Claude's assistance in a couple of things that he had run out of hands to accomplish by himself. By helping each other, they formed a bond of brotherhood.

Relda is Claude's wife. She was a troubled woman. Her physical health had worsened as she aged and her mental stability did also. Since Claude was doing so well both physically and emotionally, Relda was suspecting, in her tangled mind, that he surely had someone that he had more interest in than her.

Randy had become a Christian because Ben and Mark, the community's pastor, had taken advantage of Randy's overnight knee knocking stay in a tree house somewhere in the forest. He had earlier fathered a child with Jody. It was a girl (Sandy). That fact did not instill a true love between the two of them.

Near the end of a previous book, The Lighted Pathway, Ben had been asked to be in charge of the movements of a group of covered wagons and ox-drawn carts on a three day journey across the wide-open prairie. Was his knowledge able to get the "Prairie Schooners" safely to their destination in spite of a ferocious prairie fire that threatened their very lives? That situation opened the eyes of all those involved to the brevity of life. By this time Ben and Becky had given birth to their first child, Daniel.

Mark McKenzie was the community's Pastor. He and his wife worked with the Reeds and many others in this mostly Christian neighborhood, helping those who needed help and hope. His wife is Melinda and his two children were Nick and Savannah.

Mr. Kirkland (Kirk) was one of Nick's and Sandy's school teachers. He recently had become a Christian after he had created a situation that backed him into a corner and there discovering that his friends were not going to bail him out. Nick and Sandy were classmates.

Alvin Rush was among the old-fashioned travelers in the three day prairie crossing guided by Ben. He was the owner of one of the ox carts and the team of oxen which pulled it.

Sheriff Blake, his son Ron, a deputy, and Marvin another deputy, were quite active in their county. They worked closely with the folks in the county neighborhoods and were well respected by the whole county and outlying areas as well.

Life in this small community was not without its problems. Problems are solved much easier if the Lord is called upon to light the pathway. The best path to follow is often the narrow one.

Chapter one
Home Sweet Home

Ben brought his guitar from the bedroom. Little Daniel lay on his blanket on the living room floor with a couple of baby toys. Becky was in the kitchen, preparing an appetizing supper for Ben and herself. Ben strummed a few chords, then changed to a different set. Shortly he was humming as he strummed. Getting a piece of paper and his keepsake pencil, Ben wrote the words he was putting together in his mind. He began to play and sing the song he had written so far:

"Saved up my money and bought me a tractor, going to teach myself how to farm.

The Summer was over, the snow was now falling; I'd cut no firewood to keep myself warm.

I can't imagine where you are tonight; All that I know is, I am alone.

You seemed to have found yourself a new home; and I have no one since you have gone."

Ben pondered over words for verse two. Finally

writing them down, he gave them a try with music:

"I always thought of myself as a winner; never did like to take second place.

Then I met up with that old barnyard rooster, and now I have egg all over my face.

Why, oh why was I in a fright; and why am I still here all alone.

I was a winner when we were together; guess I was stupid, and now you are gone."

Ben heard a giggle come from the kitchen. He hadn't considered that Becky would be listening. All right, he would make a verse that could be sung in Sunday School. He thought it all out then let it rip:

"The giant just laughed when he saw David; he'd put that boy through a world of hurt.

Dave's sling went around, the smooth stone went flying; his laughter had stopped when his face hit the dirt.

Where, oh where, is his head tonight? Dave cut it off and carried it home.

Goliath, convinced that he was the champion; then he met David and now he is gone."

"Wow! That'll knock their socks off. Where did that come from?"

"Maybe I had better delete that one," Ben suggested.

"No. Don't. I doubt if it will cause anyone nightmares, and it is scriptural. Supper is ready."

Ben washed his hands, scooped up his son, placing him in his infant chair, then they joined Becky at the kitchen table.

Chapter two
Due Date/Spread the News

Sharon's due date finally came. Steven was careful to check in on his wife several times a day in the last week or two. He was hoping that they would be able to deliver at the hospital, unlike Ben and Becky who had their first baby at home. Sharon had gone through several days of pre-labor contractions. When the final ones started, there was little doubt that they were the "real McCoy". The trip to the nearest hospital was made in plenty of time. It was a journey during daylight hours and the roads were good.

About four hours later, Sharon gave birth to a seven and a half pound baby girl. Steven was present during the delivery, giving Sharon a hand to squeeze during the contractions. Later he stood close beside his wife while she cradled their daughter, and the first family photo was taken.

"Don't you need to do chores?" Sharon asked.

"Yes, I had better," Steve said. "This is more fun." He was beaming. His daughter would be as pretty as his wife; he could tell that already. "It is about sundown. I'll hurry."

"We'll be here!" Sharon assured him.

The waiting would be worth it, Steven reminded himself. He should be able to do the feeding of the cattle and horses in an hour or so, at the most.

As he got out of the car at home, Steve's ears caught a sound that was familiar to him. He waited to see if he heard it again, just to be sure. The wait was short, and Steve headed on foot in the direction from which he had heard it. A heifer was in the process of giving birth to her first calf. How long she had already struggled Steve could not tell, except for the fact that she could still stand.

Steve was able to get close enough to the wild heifer to see that two little hooves were in sight. "Lord, let there be a nose close by." During a push, Steve saw his chance to grab hold of each hoof and start pulling. Fortunately the calf's nose was positioned correctly and the mechanical pullers would probably not be necessary. With his help, the new mother soon had a new calf on the ground. Before the heifer had gotten back to her feet, Steve had made sure the calf's airway was clear and it was breathing. Placing the new baby at its mother's head, Steve left the new family to go change into his chore clothes from the nicer ones he still had on. There was precious little time left before sundown, meaning that the air would immediately start getting colder.

After a quick feeding, Steve returned to the new family. The baby was up on wobbly legs, trying to find his first meal. The heifer kept turning, trying to keep the baby at her head so she could admire her new toy.

"Stand still!" Steve said out loud, It was starting to get dark, and to Steve the mothering process was going too slowly. Because of that fact, he convinced himself that he had to act swiftly while he still had daylight. He walked hurriedly to his pickup and chose two ropes; his best one, that had a releasable Honda, and an ordinary one.

The situation was the same as Steve returned to the pair. He threw a loop over the heifer's head, then quickly tied her to a fence-line post. Using the other rope, he laid a trap loop on the ground where the heifer would walk into it. Having succeeded in that, he tied that rope to another post.

The new mother, now unable to move about, stood as Steve guided the calf to a full udder. Prying open its mouth with his fingers, he let it close on the closest source of nourishment. The calf still had enough desire to try to eat, and soon was eagerly extracting his first meal. After it had gotten a good drink of the first milk, Steve moved the calf aside so he could do the next thing in the process. What would happen then, he had misjudged. Just before releasing the loop over the heifer's head, he untied the rope from the post holding the back leg. When freed from the head rope, the heifer took off through the pasture. She never looked back at her new calf, but kept going, eventually stepping out of the leg loop.

At that time Steve took off running in a wide circle to the opposite side of the heifer, and in a few minutes was turning her back toward her calf. As both of them were getting close to where they ought to be, Steve saw that the heifer had her eyes and intentions on the open gate to sixty acres of wheat pasture.

"No!" Steve thought as he took off running again. He not only had to close the distance between him and the heifer, but also get in front of her to block the opening. The cold air going into his lungs made them hurt, but this was no time to worry about that. Fortunately the heifer was still weak enough, and Steve fast enough, that he barely won that race. He stood in the gate opening, hands on his knees for support, watching as the heifer again wandered back toward the same pasture they had just come from. His energy was spent.

"Lord, I give up!" Steve prayed. He remembered what his friend Ben had said about hopeless situations, and knew it was true for all who believe in God's mercy. In line with all that, he breathed out what he knew to be true. "All things work together for good to those who love (trust) the Lord; to those who are the called according to His purpose." Then he prayed the faith words that must follow: "Thank you, Jesus for this situation which I have lost control of. I don't know what to do next. Thank you anyway for the good that only you can send."

The sun had set. The damp cold air was gathering, first in the low spots, then quickly to the rest of the area. Steve had his second wind even though he was not ready for another race. He looked at his heifer. What he saw, he only hoped were true. His wild animal was walking toward the barn, which was about a hundred fifty yards away. No other cattle were even near the barn. Steve followed at a distance, on foot at a walking pace, watching the heifer not only go into the pen south of the barn, but literally go into the barn through the already open door. He was praising God as he latched the door. All he had left to do was to bring the calf to its mama.

Walking back to the calf, Steve leaned over and putting one arm behind the calf's back legs and at the same time the other arm in front of the front legs just below the calf's neck, he gathered up his load and proceeded toward the barn. With each step the calf seemed to be gaining weight. Steve's arms were hurting as he opened the door to the barn and placed the calf into the darkness.

"Take care of him," Steve said as he once again latched the door. He would check on them later. For now, he had someone he wanted to get back to, his wife and new daughter.

After his shower and donning a fresh set of clothes, Steve ignored the fact that he had not eaten since breakfast. On the road again, Steve felt the hunger, but reminded himself that that could come later also.

"You were gone a long time," Sharon said. "Did you have problems?"

"Yes, and no," Steve related the whole story to his wife. Both of them were in tears as Steve finished his story and marveled at the "grace of God" on this perfect day.

"With that in mind," Sharon reminded Steve, "We have not yet officially named our daughter. Of all the names we were proposing, could we just name her………

"Grace?" Steve asked, not waiting for Sharon to finish.

"Would that be all right?" Sharon asked.

"I would say it was perfect," Steve beamed, "And could we use your middle name as hers also?"

"Grace Elaine. Yes, I do believe we are ready to close this case, your Honor." The new parents both laughed so heartily that a nurse came into the room, wondering what could be so funny. Then Sharon stated, "I need to call Becky. She will want to celebrate with us, I know."

"My friend in the mountains would have liked to know all this too. Maybe some day. Maybe some day." After Grace Elaine had gotten her first meal, Steve knew that he should excuse himself and go home again. "See you later, Grace Elaine."

"Don't forget me!"

"I will never forget you!" Steve promised. "In fact I will probably be driving you home in as couple of days, I would say."

After he got home, Steve only went to the house long enough to get a big flashlight. The barn did not have lights even though it had two grain rooms, stanchions and a hay loft. Arriving at the barn, Steve shined the light through one of the many gaps between the siding boards. In front of the narrow beam of light stood the heifer, half way across barn, and the baby which was getting, at least, its second meal.

"Not only grace," Steve thought, "But amazing grace." It was much more than "a sweet sound."

****

Becky answered her ringing phone. "Hello." Her caller ID showed "unlisted number".

"Beck, this is Sharon. I need to lean on you again."

Becky sat bolt upright in bed. "Oh,oh! What is wrong?"

"Well, this afternoon I began to feel quite uncomfortable, so Steve ran me in to the hospital."

"And?"

"The baby.......came out."

"Oh no!"

"Oh yes! We named her Grace Elaine."

"She is OK?"

"She was a bit noisy for a few minutes, but she is sleeping quietly at the moment."

"Sharon, you are a pill. What do you need me for?"

"I need you to come congratulate me; or rather, us."

"You bet! I'll tell Ben."

"Don't come tonight. I will still be here all day tomorrow. Rather, we will be here all day tomorrow."

"Grace Elaine. With a name like that, she has to be a pretty baby."

"She is perfect. I counted her fingers and she is only two short of a full dozen. The strange thing, her toes are too."

"Ah, what a shame." They both laughed. "Ben wants to know what is so funny. I had better tell him so he can go back to sleep."

"What time is it?"

"A quarter past eleven."

"I'm sorry. I woke you."

"I will recover. This is today's news. I had to hear it today."

"Steve has something to tell also. We will catch you on that tomorrow."

"Thanks. Good night."

"Good night."

Ben was still awake.

"Steve and Sharon have a little girl."

"Wonderful!"

"Can we go see them tomorrow?"

"After sun-up I hope."

"Let's say, after Daniel wakes up."

"OK, Goodnight."

Chapter three
Shaken

Claude got an early start one morning in his "beef taxi". He had contracted three loads of calves to be delivered to a neighborhood feedlot. While on his way out of town, he met Ben who was on his way into town. Ben had not talked to Claude for some time so he called him just to say "howdy". Howdy was not all they would talk about, however. Before the call ended, Claude commented, "Looks like a fire ahead of me. Can't tell yet what is burning." As he drew closer, he saw a dehydrator on a natural gas line was on fire. He told Ben, and just as he was about to say "goodbye," he shouted, "Call for help! Got a man on fire! I'll see what I can do!"

Claude quickly brought his rig to a halt, and after grabbing a blanket from his sleeper, vaulted to the ground and ran toward the man. By then the fire on the man had gone out. All the clothing he had left on was his underwear bottom and a cuff on his right wrist that had probably been a part of a light jacket. Shielding the man from a chilly north breeze with the blanket, Claude offered to cover him with the blanket.

The man, now on his hands and knees, said, "I'm not cold." Ribbons of blistered skin hung from the man's chest, stomach and arms. Claude laid part of the blanket on the ground beside the man. The fellow started to lay down on it, but probably because of pain got back up on his hands and knees.

Ben had made a fast u-turn, and while heading toward the fire, made his call to 911 for help. He looked at his speedometer just before slowing down for the stop at the fire and read 85 under the speedometer arm. It hardly seemed he was going fast at all. As he joined Claude, Ben saw the man's condition. Not a hair was left on him; on his upper half, at least: no eyebrows, no eyelashes, no whiskers, and a completely bald head.

"Help is on the way!" Ben announced. He noticed that the man had on a wedding band. "We had better remove the ring before your hand begins to swell." The man raised his hand up to Ben who took the ring off his finger. Having no better place to put it, Ben stuck it into his own pocket.

The sheriff department car soon pulled to a stop at the scene and a deputy came carrying a yellow burn-victim blanket. Also in his hand he carried a bottle of water, which he gave to the victim. Through parched lips, the man took a small drink. "The ambulance is about five minutes behind me." It seemed like ten minutes before it got there. Ben had handed the man's ring to the deputy who put it into his own pocket.

Sheriff Blake himself pulled up just seconds before the ambulance. Claude and Ben, seeing that they were not needed any more, went to their vehicles and left. They would both be contacted later for their eyewitness statements. A gas man arrived to shut off the appropriate valve to stop the gas flow to the fire, which having burned an area of at least forty yards in diameter, was now limited to the dehydrator. It was only then, as Ben was driving away from the scene, that he realized that he had not even asked God's presence or guidance over the situation. That thought made him feel ashamed of himself. He apologized to God for his tardiness and then asked for divine care for the victim, whatever his name. Somehow names hadn't mattered at the moment, and surely God knew what needed to done before anyone called upon Him for help.

Chapter four
Called

After hearing Ben tell her of his day, Becky felt a strong urge to be helping someone herself. She did not know who or how. Maybe it was just that Ben had done good and she had wanted to have done something useful. Claude called to talk to Ben as he was delivering his last load of calves. It was then that Becky knew who she was feeling compelled to go see. She told Ben. "I don't know why, but I feel drawn to go see Relda. Can you watch Daniel?"

"That would be better than what I had planned to do. I was going to cut some dead wood, but I had better get this fire out of my head before I pick up my chain saw. I will be right there. We will go looking for dead trees together." When Ben got home, he took Daniel. Becky got ready and went to town.

After Becky introduced herself at Relda's front door, she had the dreadful feeling that the door was about to be shut in her face. Finally, Relda opened the door wider while unenthusiastically announcing, "Well, come in then."

Not knowing how to properly start a conversation, Becky shared with Relda the feeling that she felt she was sent there.

"You guys and your God!" Relda blurted out, while rolling her eyes and closing the door. Becky had not even mentioned God at this point. "What enchanted thing did he tell you to tell me?"

Becky so much felt like saying, "I don't know!" and then leave. She knew; however, that God would never send anyone to an unsuccessful mission. "What do I say now?" Becky prayed silently.

"The truth," it seemed God was saying.

"He wants me to tell you that He loves you." She knew that was the truth, and that was always a good place to start. "How are you doing……really?"

"You don't want to know!" Relda blurted.

"Why not?"

"Because you are so, so blessed, for lack of a better word, and I am so at the bottom of……..nowhere."

"Then that is probably why I was sent here."

"To rub my face in it?"

"No, to tell you that God has a wonderful plan for your life."

"If your book says that, then why haven't I read it?"

"Maybe because you read it with criticism instead of faith?" Becky said, still not sure of what direction to continue the conversation. It was Relda that was now paving the way in this discussion. Could that mean that under Relda's attitude of gloom and despair there was a hunger that even she had not recognized?"

Relda suddenly stood and left the room. Becky wasn't sure what that was suppose to mean. Soon she came back and tossed a dusty Bible on the coffee table in front of Becky.

"Show me!" Relda challenged. "There is no Relda anywhere in there."

Becky had the urge to dust off the Bible before she opened it, but wisely supposed that would be an insult to Relda. She instinctively turned to the book of John. "Here it is!" Relda leaned curiously toward Becky, who handed the Bible to her while pointing to John 3:16. After Relda read it, she looked up at Becky. "Couldn't the word, whosoever, be easily replaced with Relda, to read, 'If Relda believes in Him, she will not perish, but have everlasting life?' And look at John 1:12, 'As Relda believes in Him to her gave he the power to become a daughter of God'. Of course, this all comes through faith. Look at this: 'He who comes to God must believe that He is, and that He is a rewarder of them who diligently seek Him'." Becky turned some more pages. "Here is another one."

Relda read aloud, "God hath given unto us eternal life; this life is in His Son. He who hath the Son, hath life; He who hath not the Son of God, hath not life."

Becky was sensing that the coldness toward her was melting, and with God's power, a real warmth could develop. "It is not a necessarily easy life. Jesus said, 'In this world you will have tribulation, but be of good cheer, I have overcome the world'. Recently it was pointed out to me that Jesus prayed for you and me to the Father." Becky turned to the seventeenth chapter of John and showed Relda.

After she read it, Relda admitted, "Yeah, that could be for us. What do we do to get on his good side?"

Becky knew what Relda meant by that question. "Let's see what he requires." She turned to Revelation 3:20 and as Relda looked on, read, "Behold, I stand at the door and knock. If any man, or woman," Becky added, "Should hear my voice and open the door, I will come in and sup with him, and he with me." She also knew the best verses to show someone that they couldn't get to Heaven by their own power: Ephesians 2:8-9.

Relda read those two verses, then asked, "Then what the plan?"

Becky found John chapter 14. She read the conversation Jesus had with Thomas emphasizing: "I am the Way, the Truth, and the Life; no man cometh unto the Father except by Me."

"What about all those other religions? Are they all wrong?"

"It all comes down to what we just read. Believe the truth and we will have the power to live it. Don't believe, and continue in hopelessness."

As Relda got to her feet in front of the divan, she said, "Come here a minute." She led Becky into the kitchen. On the table were several containers of medicine, and a large full glass of water.

"I didn't mean to disrupt your medication schedule," Becky apologized.

"I..was going to try to take them all. My intent was to pass out before I quit. I was hating everyone and everything. God was included in what I hated for letting me live like this. Are you sure that He has made a way for people as pathetic as me?"

Becky wanted to get both of them out of the kitchen. She motioned for Relda to follow her back to the living room. Seated again on the divan, Becky opened the word to Romans 3:23. After Relda read that verse, Becky showed her 6:23. At that point Relda took the Bible from Becky and started searching on her own. Becky noticed that Relda was starting at chapter five of Romans. She did not stop until she got to the end of chapter six. She looked up at Becky, then back to the chapter five page. She read these words softly, "But God commended His love toward us in that while we were yet sinners, Christ died for us."

"Now turn to chapter ten," Becky directed. "Now read, starting at verse nine." Relda kept reading for some time. She was holding the Bible in such a position that Becky was unable to read along with her. Becky closed her eyes and silently interceded for Relda. She opened her eyes just after Relda brushed her hand across the open pages of the Bible. She wondered why Relda had done that, until she looked at her face. Great tears were flowing; one had landed on God's word, the word Relda was just now cherishing for the very first time.

"May I pray for you?" Becky asked.

"Please!" Relda quickly said.

Becky placed her hands over Relda's and prayed all the words that God was giving her. As she was coming to the end of her intercession, Relda began her own heart-felt plea. She dumped loads at the cross, thanking God for their removal. She gave a big sigh. "Is this the God that Claude believes in?"

"The same!" Becky told her. "Is he coming home tonight?"

"Is this Saturday?"

"Yes, it is."

"He will be here....got church tomorrow. Do you think he would mind a passenger going with him?"

"You may have to drive. He might not be able to watch the road."

"Guess I had better put the pills away and get supper ready. He should be pulling in soon. And I had better wash off these tears. He might think I am sad." They both chuckled. "Can we get together again soon?"

"I would like that! How about supper at our house Sunday evening?"

"If he can. Sure! We will!"

Becky drove home to prepare a meal for her big man and her little man. Her feeling had been satisfied. Was this a dream? No, it was a miracle; a miracle of God's love.

Chapter five
Differences

"Mr. Reed?" the voice on the phone asked.

"Yes, this is he."

The caller continued, "This is the grade school principal. I am new to the district this year. I doubt that we have met."

"No, but we probably will some day."

"Mr. Reed, the reason I am calling is because of a new reading program we are introducing this year. We are asking business men and women to donate a little of their time to read a story to the younger students. The group would consist of those in kindergarten through second grades. Since you work with nature in the great outdoors, you have been considered an excellent candidate for this project."

"I am interested. Do I pick the topic, and how long should it be?"

"If you will read for up to ten minutes, that would be great; and if you could enlighten the kids on range plants or animals and how they came to be over the years; well, you pick the teaching avenue. Could you come in next Monday shortly before one o'clock?"

"Barring some emergency, I will be there." Ben later told Becky about the matter.

"Does it seem that he has an agenda?" Becky asked.

"I couldn't tell. He talked about nature and how things came to be over the years, which I could take as his push for evolution, but he never came right out and said so. I intend to do it my way. I wasn't asked to show him the material for his approval. Maybe he assumed that his suggestions would steer me in the 'progressive' direction."

"What are you reading to them?"

"I have only begun to think about that. I believe that a little fiction to prove a point won't hurt a thing." Becky was silent, hoping Ben would elaborate. He did, a little. "They will be the first to hear about the albino cougar."

"The albino cougar? Is there such a thing?"

"That is my little secret, but it will be interesting to see if I can convince them enough to get my point across."

"Which is?"

"Differences are not always good and not always bad, or something like that."

"Now you have me interested. Don't scare them too badly."

Ben chuckled and went to get his old high school clipboard and some notebook paper. Becky watched as Ben wrote. She could tell that he was enjoying himself. He kept writing as if he already had the story memorized. Did her Ben have an undiscovered ability to write fiction?

His skill of writing about his mountain adventure already showed he could write about real life.

On Monday, Ben came in at noon; to eat a meal and to clean up for his trip to town. Becky had successfully resisted the urge to read Ben's story before he presented it to the children.

****

At school, the principal escorted Ben to the reading room. The children were seated in chairs arranged in a semicircle. They were in awe of Ben as he walked in, wearing his finest forest ranger outfit.

After being introduced by the principal, Ben greeted them. "Hi kids!"

"Hi, Ranger Reed!" the children chorused. They had apparently rehearsed that greeting.

Ben began this way. "It is an honor to be here with you today. Some of you may be thinking that you are about to hear some old familiar story. You have never heard this one, because it has not yet been told. This story is about an albino cougar. Do you know what a cougar is?" One hand shot up.

"Yes?"

"A mountain lion." The boy knew that for certain.

"That is right. And what is albino?"

A girl stated matter-of-factly, "It is white!"

"How did you know that?" Ben asked her.

"We have a albino catfish in our pond."

"You do? We have some in one pond out on the

range too. Now to my story. For years a man named Reuben told about seeing an all-white cougar. The town folk did not believe one word of it right away. That fact did not stop Reuben from sticking to his story. This is how he told his story: 'One morning while out on the range, just before sun-up, I heard a big cat growl. I quickly turned to see bright white as it disappeared into the underbrush. I waited a few minutes until daylight, then went to where I had caught a glimpse of the white creature. I couldn't see any paw prints of the mountain lion so it must have been a phantom. From the height of the white I had seen, the cat must have been three feet tall, or maybe even four.' About that same time, several ranchers had been losing calves; some of them over two hundred pounds. Reuben would remind them that it must be the albino. People began flocking to the range with cameras and guns. The guns were unauthorized, and were confiscated, but that did not stop the frenzy. The stories enlarged to the point that even the people in nearby towns were in fear of their children's safety and of their own."

"'Our livestock and our pets are in danger!' the people were saying. 'The cougar has to resort to killing tame animals for his food, since he has a hard time sneaking up on wild prey because of its color. There is no telling what it will do next or where. He's got a demon,' some began to say. 'He is crazed to kill, not just to eat.'"

"Doesn't this all seem possible?" Ben asked the kids. Several of them nodded. "Now I ask you, don't we sometimes do the same thing with people as they did the white mountain lion? You probably have fellow classmates who are shorter than most of the others and possibly some taller or larger than the rest. Other children look different in other ways. Remember this: God made you all. You are not carbon copies of each other nor would you want to be. Since we are made by a loving God with individual design, we have no reason or right to make fun of, or make up stories about the different children. That would be no way to win them for Jesus. He died for them all."

"The albino cougar was called a vicious freak. Let's back up and get the facts. Reuben never actually saw the big cat. The white he saw was probably the tail of a deer which an ordinary cougar might have been chasing. No one saw one eating cattle or pets, or kids. It was all a bad story promoted by fear and imagination. Truthfully, I don't believe a single word of the tale. As for your friends, be a friend, not an enemy. We are actually all different. That is my story for today. I was glad to share it with you. Learn all you can today, and make your story a true one."

The principal thanked Ben for coming. The teachers took the children to their rooms.

"I was afraid you were going to start preaching," the principal told Ben.

"Is next Monday open?"

"No!" the principal was quick to reply.

"Why are you afraid?"

"Law suits," the principal said forcefully

"I suspect two things. First, you are not familiar with the law; second, you have not yet accepted Jesus as your Savior. Am I right?"

"I don't have to answer either one,"

"Here is the answer for the first," Ben handed the principal a copy of the state law concerning religion in the classroom. "Concerning the second, I would enjoy showing you from the Bible what God requires from each of us."

"I suppose you espouse life after death?"

"Yes, and in addition to that, if I handed you my gun and you shot me, I would not die."

"We'll see about that this!" and then he turned to briskly walk to his office.

Ben walked out of the school, back to his pickup and drove home. Maybe, he told himself, it might have been better if he had not mentioned God.

That evening Becky read Ben's story and he filled the unwritten part about his conversation with the principal.

"Did you show him your gun?"

"I didn't take it. Do you suppose he thought I had one with me?"

Ben's question was answered later that evening when the president of the school board called.

"You didn't take your gun to school. Tell me you didn't."

"I didn't," Ben told him. "He must have wanted to believe I did. He was looking for a way to discredit me. He was afraid I was going to convert the children to Christianity, it appeared."

"Did he know you could talk about God, since you were invited to speak?"

"He does now. I gave him a copy of the state law

after I saw that he must have been misinformed about it. I never had an altar call. I just encouraged the kids to be kind to the other kids even if they may look different, because God made them too."

The board president added. "I was wondering what kind of man we were hiring for the job. He was a little too pompous to suit me, but he had all the right credentials. We need to pray for him."

"I am thrilled to hear you say that. I offered to meet with him privately and show him hope from the Bible. At that point, he turned his back on me and left."

"Well, I guess you won't need to prepare a new story to read. I doubt you'll be asked back."

"Not until he has a heart change." The two men finished their conversations and goodbyes.

Chapter six
Timber!

"Shouldn't you just let it go?" Becky asked.

"Probably." Ben looked up at his wife. How did she know what he was thinking?

"Will you?" Becky had observed Ben since he got home from reading to the school children, and especially after his talk with the school board president. He leaned over to his wife and gave her a quick kiss, then got up from the divan to get ready for bed.

"Not yet; maybe later," he told her. Ben took his evening shower, but instead of going immediately to bed, he rejoined Becky in the living room. Picking up the latest daily newspaper, he scanned through it, trying to get his mind on other matters. None of the names in the obits were anyone he knew, and the comics were no longer comical. Editorials, except for the local ones, were slanted mostly to the left; some with a vengeance. Finally, Ben said goodnight and headed to bed.

"I will be there shortly. I'm about to finish this one."

She was working a crossword puzzle in an earlier newspaper issue.

Ben must have been concentrating on the principal's words too long, and what he could have said to him. He even dreamed about it that night. Part of the dream seemed so real. He remembered that part the next day and wondered if it had any merit for things to come.

Ben scheduled himself a day each week to drive all the main roads of the range just to check the range condition and to see if poachers were breaking range laws. As usual, this morning's drive revealed no surprises. All was well; he ended his drive at his range office. At his desk, Ben looked at his phone, but instead of reaching for it, he folded his hands and closed his eyes. "God, why is this so heavy on my heart? I hardly know the guy. Why should it matter to me what he believes or what his hang-ups are? Daniel has several more years before he goes to school. This man may be gone by then. If I am suppose to go see him again, you send me. That is the only way it will work anyway." Ben ended his prayer at that point. He made some notes in his Ranger's Log, then went outside.

How did people in their lives find out about God's love for them? Becky had earlier felt drawn to Relda's house and arrived just before Relda would have swallowed the drugs that she had calculated would have brought her death. Mack was called to his son's teacher's house by the teacher himself. Randy was stranded in a tree house, of sorts, while Mack led him to the Lord from fifteen feet below. Mr. Robinson got a prayer answered before he even trusted God. Marvin saw a drama of the death and resurrection of Christ, and believed. There was no set pattern, but God had a plan for each of them. The school principal was in God's plan too. Ben could feel it, and was eager to be a part of it. Several times he wanted to give Howard (the principal) a call but felt it was his own zeal that was driving him, not God.

****

For most of this day, Ben spent his time and energy in locating downed dead trees, then pulling them to spots where people could cut them into firewood length and then take them home. The next day Ben would have an ad put in the local paper announcing the availability of the trees and the time limitation for firewood removal. He remembered what the turnout of firewood cutters were for previous years. He was certain that he had as much or more trees available this year, and located in three spots. The ad would be in the next Friday's paper. The first Saturday after the ad was published usually proved to be the busiest day. It reminded Ben of the first day of any hunting season.

On Saturday morning, eleven vehicles drove in and parked at the range office. Ben had them wait until nine A.M. before he would start escorting them to the cutting sites. Fifteen chain saws would be in action. Ben made his assignments by passing out sticky notes to the guys with a 1, 2, or 3 written on them.

Just as they were pulling out to go to the sites, a latecomer came up the driveway. Ben put his arm out of the window of his old red pickup and motioned for the latest to follow along. The driver waved; he understood. In the last vehicle, which was a car pulling a small trailer, there was only one person. The assignments were evened out, four at each location. It reminded Ben of a story he heard several years ago from one of the firewood cutters. The story went like this: A local Indian in a certain part of the northern states was asked what the approaching winter was going to be like. The Indian's words were few but decisive.

"Winter very cold and long." The word passed fast and soon there was a frenzy of firewood collectors. After so long a time, one curious fellow asked the old Indian just how he knew the winter would be long and cold. The old fellow did not make a long story about crops or animal fur or any other common signs. He just took a sip of his coffee and said, "Many white man make big piles of firewood." Ben chuckled as he recalled the story.

Ben assigned the number 1's to the first spot, and similarly the 2's to the second, and the 3's to the last. "I will come by at times to see how you are doing," he told them. At spot three, Ben got a close look at the last arriver. He was the school principal, Howard Zerger. Ben hoped the man knew how to handle a saw. He noticed that the saw was brand new.

Soon the woods were ringing with two-cycled motors. It was a good day for the operation. Ben had a fourth spot in mind to get his own winter's supply. He opted to do his on a day when he wasn't checking on these that came today. Most of the workers had on leather shoes of some sort. That was good. A few of the boys had basketball shoes, but hopefully their jobs would be that of loading the wood onto vehicles.

Occasionally shouts of, "Timber!" was heard as workers finished the cuts on limbs not already lying one the ground. Fun or not, it was a good lumberjack practice. Howard immediately decided that he need not enter into such childish prattle. By thinking thusly, he also ignored the others who enjoyed seeing how often they could say it. One time he was halfway through a cut when the closest fellow to him bellowed out a "Timber!" and shortly followed it with a louder, "Look out!"

"Such nonsense," Howard muttered, then his world went dark.

Ben took his first drive out to check on the firewood cutters. He took a glance at groups one and two, as he drove on to group three. The first two groups were busy as beavers. Group three seemed to be silent. "Group water break," Ben thought. As he came into better view of group three, he noticed that the guys were in a huddle. "Oh, oh," Ben said aloud and silently thought, "Someone is hurt."

One of the fellows from group three saw Ben's pickup approaching and ran out to meet him. He was shouting. "Get help!" he yelled, and said something about "Hospital."

Ben grabbed his cell and called the EMT's. "Ranger Reed...got one man hurt, need a wagon, fast...Ranger Station...meet you there!" He pulled to a stop beside group three's spot. One fellow was lying under a large limb, out cold. His head was lying on top of another limb, his neck at an odd angle. Ben barked orders on where to place sawn logs, then backed his pickup near to the injured man. He pulled out his log chain, instructed a fellow where to attach it to the limb, then he fastened the other end to his truck.

"Stand clear!" he screamed as he literally jumped into Rover and ground it into gear. The pickup lurched forward. The limb came off the body and landed on top of the cut logs, leaving the body free.

"Got a pulse!" one guy yelled. "Bleeding out his nose and mouth!"

"I'll get the EMT's," Ben yelled. "Don't roll him onto his back; he'll drown."

The ambulance pulled into the driveway as Ben got to the office. He motioned and spun around heading back to spot three. The EMT's followed. The guys at spot one and two shut off all saws and watched as the two vehicles shot by them. They decided not to start cutting again, but to finish loading what they had already cut.

As the ambulance took Howard to the hospital twenty miles away, Ben saw that all cutting had stopped. He shouted, "Thank you! Load and go! He is alive, yet!" The guys nodded then continued loading.

Ben called Becky and Mark. He stopped at the office to get Howard's phone number. It wasn't in the book yet, but information found it for him. He called Howard's home before he got on the open highway. He assumed Howard was married. He didn't know for sure.

"Hello," the lady's voice answered.

"Hello, this is Ranger Reed. Is your husband Howard?"

"Yes, he is. What....."

"There has been an accident. Howard is hurt. He is on his way to the hospital."

"Driving?"

"No, by ambulance. Want me to take you?"

"No, I'll come. Told him the saw would get him."

"It didn't. He is not cut. A limb got him."

"I will hurry."

"Be careful," Ben cautioned.

"K"

Ben realized he was driving old Rover. He opted to get the newer pickup before going on to the hospital. Mark got to the hospital before Ben. Mrs. Zerger arrived after both of them.

"How is he?" Mrs. Zerger asked.

"We don't know," Mark told her. "We are praying."

"Praying," she said. "I should have known. Have you seen him? Can I see him?"

"No, we haven't, and not before a doctor or a nurse tells us. You first, or course."

"What happened?"

Ben filled Howard's wife in with the edited version of the story, not mentioning that Howard purposely ignored the warnings. At this time Ben's phone rang. Becky's number appeared. "Hi. We are at the hospital. His wife is here."

"Is she a believer?"

"Nothing yet indicates that."

"You and Mark have been praying, I know. Does she know?"

"Yes, and yes; got poo-pooed sort of, when we told her."

"Sad. I'll start the chain. (prayer chain)"

"Good!"

Finally a doctor came into the waiting room. "Mark, Ben. Are you Mrs. Zerger?"

"Yes. May I see him?"

"Yes, but first I must tell you, he is totally sedated. There seems to be no large blood loss or cranial pools. Sometimes, after a thump like this, there is." Mark and Ben exchanged smiles. The doctor saw and understood. He had heard several times about their faith. "Come with me," the doctor told Mrs. Zerger. "Don't touch his head." She followed the doctor to Howard's bedside. "There's a cranial crack on this side. He will be monitored around the clock. Here is a chair, if you want to stay with him."

"Thanks. I do."

"A nurse will be in to get information, insurance and things like that. Do you want a chaplain?"

"I think I have two already. Don't see that another one would help."

"OK." The doctor left the room, and on his way to another patient, stopped to inform Mark and Ben all he knew about Howard's condition, so far. A nurse entered the emergency room with several forms to be filled out by Mrs. Zerger.

"I'll stay tonight, if you want to go," Mark told Ben.

"You have church tomorrow. Don't want you

falling asleep during the sermon like I do," Ben cracked.

"One of us should, for her sake."

"I'm willing," Ben told him.

"Then I will be back after church tomorrow."

"Don't come without eating. He will be here for awhile, I am thinking."

Howard was kept sedated all night, but was allowed an opportunity to awaken at daylight the next day.

"Zan?" Howard mumbled.

Jan quickly awoke in her chair and sprang to her feet. "I'm here, Howard," she told him.

"Ospidle?" Howard asked.

"Yes, hospital." She pressed the call button. A nurse was already entering the room.

"Good morning, Mr. Zerger!" the nurse greeted.

"Unh." a good enough greeting for now. The doctor entered in a few seconds.

"We doing better?" the doctor asked.

"God a fog in, pogget? I ert"

"You will feel as good as me and my frog in a few days. As for the match between you and the tree, the tree won the first round. I can see you getting even with it some day."

"Dimber," the hurting man said, trying to smile. He closed his eyes for a little bit. When he opened them, he had a question. "Wanger come?"

"Wanger?" Jan asked.

"Wanger Weed," Howard said.

"I will get him," the nurse said. She went to the waiting room and told Ben that Howard was asking for him.

"I figured I was the last one he would want to see."

The nurse's eyes asked, "Why?"

"Long story." He followed the nurse to Howard's bedside. Jan moved a little, so that Ben could get closer to Howard. The doctor spoke a little more with Jan and then left the room.

"Mornin' lumberjack."

"Morn' Ben," Howard forced himself to say. "God a zermon for me?"

"Not until I am sure you won't go to sleep while I preach it," Ben said, smiling.

"Mide do that. Lader?"

"I will be back tomorrow. Got to fine tune it so you won't be bored." Howard tried to chuckle; couldn't hardly. Howard reached out a hand. Ben took it and gave it a squeeze. The deal was made. Jan was confused. The two men weren't, however.

Mark was coming into the hospital as Ben was leaving. Ben filled him in.

"Good!" Mark said. "I will visit awhile, then go home. I won't upstage you. God gave this mission to you." He visited a little while with Jan. Howard had drifted back into sleep. Jan did allow Mark to pray for her and Howard, and to escort her to the lunch room for her first meal since she got there.

"What are you going to tell him?" Becky asked Ben that evening.

"I don't know yet. It will come, it always has. I probably won't mention the albino cougar."

"Good plan, I think," Becky said and grinned.

"I missed church."

"If he is awake tomorrow, you will have church."

****

Monday morning, Ben got ready and left early for the trip to the hospital. Howard was awake when Ben entered the room. Jan chose to step out to wait in the waiting room.

"How you doing?"

"Head throbs a little. Medicine probably keeps it from hurting a lot."

"Sometimes pain is good."

"I see you brought your Bible. Whatcha got for me?"

"What do you want?"

"I want to know why I am still alive. How close did I come to not being?"

"About this close," Ben said, showing a quarter-inch between his finger and thumb. And as for why, God is merciful, and He is jealous to not let anyone have you for eternity, besides himself, of course."

"Why?"

"Would He care that much? It is His nature. God is love. If He knew that you would not ever reach for Him. I believe you would be in a box instead of a bed."

"Fill me in. What is my sin? What are my chances? What must I do?"

"Whoa! One question at a time! I will answer these three the best I can, with His help. You inherited your first sin by being a human being, a descendant of Adam. The rest you found on your own. Your chances are zilch, if you are depending on your self worth. You created nothing. You control very little. You cannot stop time. You can't calm a storm, or for that matter, stop a falling tree branch. And unless God draws you toward himself, you cannot even come to him. Now for some of the words of hope:" Ben opened the Bible, praying that the right verses would come to mind as fast as Howard could drink them in.

"For God so loved the world that He gave His only begotten Son; that whosoever believes in Him shall not perish, but have everlasting life." Ben turned some pages, not even looking at Howard. "God has given us eternal life; this life is in His Son. He who has the Son has life; He who has not the Son of God has not life." Ben kept turning pages and reading, "All have sinned and come short of the glory of God. There is none righteous; no not one. He who says that he has no sin has made God a liar. Perchance a man would give his life for a righteous man, but God commended His love toward us in that while we were yet sinners, Christ died for us. He came unto His own and His own received Him not, but as many as received Him, to them gave He power to become the sons of God."

"Jesus told His disciples that they knew the way to eternal life. They still asked Him to show them the way. He said 'I am the way, the truth and the life; no man cometh unto the Father, but by me!'"

"Stop!" Howard said.

Ben finally took his eyes from his Bible to look at Howard. Howard's tears were flooding down the sides of his face, soaking the pillow he was lying on.

"I want to see the last verse you read for myself."

Ben held his Bible so that Howard could see where he had already highlighted the verse. "John fourteen, verse six," he told Howard.

"Oh God!" Howard said, after reading. He looked at Ben and asked, "What do I need to do to receive everlasting life?"

Ben turned to the book of Acts and found the place where the jailer asked Paul and Silas the same question. He showed Howard. Howard wiped some tears from his eyes so he could see to read, then he read aloud, "Believe on the Lord Jesus Christ and thou shalt be saved, and thy house."

"Ben, I now have no doubt that Jesus died for me. He took my sin. He told me by the words you and I read."

"You are telling me; tell Him."

Howard didn't have any hesitation. "God," he said with a penitent voice. "Thank you for calling me and dying for me, and rising from the dead, and going to make a place for me, and coming for me when it is my time to go."

Ben knew that the Holy Spirit was at work. Howard was loosely quoting verses that he had not yet read. After some time in prayer Howard said, "Go get Jan. She needs to know."

Ben left his Bible at Howard's side and stepped out to get Jan. When they came back together, Ben saw that Howard had reopened the Bible and had it laid over his heart. His eyes were closed.

"Thank you, Jesus. Thank you Jesus," Howard was saying, then he noticed Jan standing beside him. "Jan, He is real. He loves me; he loves you."

"I'll get the nurse!" Jan said in a panic.

Howard gripped her arm. "No, Jan! I am not delusional. I'm giddy, but not delusional. Ben I want a Bible just like yours."

"I will get you one." Mark and Becky would want to know. He would call them later.

Chapter seven
Comparing Beliefs

After the prairie fire incident, Alvin Rush discovered that he had become a sort of stranger in his extended family. His wife, Alice, understood her husband and why he had changed. She had earlier all but given up hope that she would see the day when Alvin would actively seek the Lord's will. In her family, there was a wait-and-see attitude concerning Alvin's newfound religion. Neither Alvin nor Alice forced their faith onto either side of the family. Theirs wasn't the pushy kind of faith to begin with, and both of them knew time was a better teacher than quick nudges.

Alice use to always do her Bible reading while Alvin was out of the house. And even at that, she never did it very often. Now, however, she often saw him reading his Bible, the first one he'd ever owned. Alice resisted the urge to get her Bible and quickly join him, wondering if that would seem too pushy. She was hoping that something would spark a family devotion time, but promised herself that she would be patient. The right time would come. Alvin would lay the corner stone by somehow inviting her to read a passage or look up something. For now, her heart was warmed by watching him. The prairie fire had an impact on all the Schooners, but it was Ben's leadership that directed the proper attitudes and guided hearts to seek the Lord. Had Ben wanted to, he could have hogged all the glory for himself. Of course he didn't, nor did he want to. Setting backfires was one of the things he had learned in ranger school several years ago. He had also remembered reading about it in a library book he had checked out in high school.

Not long after the range incident, a couple of men from a neighboring state came to the Rush's door to talk about their religion. Alice let them in only because Alvin was at home at the time. News of the fire had reached that church, and also the story of the ox-drawn carts in the three-day run.

"Our people crossed this great land in ox carts," one of the men said as an opener to their planned conversation. They were pushing west to a place where they could settle, where they could build homes and families."

"We have our own religion," Alvin told the men, presuming that was their purpose for the visit. "How is yours different or better than ours?" He was already convinced enough in his own relationship to God to feel confident in asking, just out of curiosity.

"Our founder," the second man explained, "Got a revelation from God from some ancient writings he had found and translated. In deciphering the writings, he saw that God had a new and a better plan for his people. We were chosen to spread that new plan along with the new hope. We now know that Christ was a great prophet in his day and is now a God over His People."

"Are saying Jesus was at one time just an ordinary man?"

"I couldn't have said it better. This book can explain it better than I am able to in the time we can spend with you this evening. I will leave you a free copy and a guide to show you where to find answers to the questions most people ask."

Alvin had heard a little about that religion. He tried to remember some of what he had heard, so he could ask the right questions. "Did Jesus have brothers and sisters?"

"Oh yes! One of the brothers was a rebel of sorts. He was always jealous of Jesus, the favored one. He is still this day trying to attain the following that Jesus has."

"So Jesus became a god and the other brother didn't?"

"Yes, and greater news is that we can be forgiven and follow in Jesus' footsteps." The man mistook Alvin's curiosity and learned questions as being fertile ground to plant a 'deeper truth'.

"To where?" Alvin asked.

"To godhood!"

"That's different!" Alvin exclaimed, then excused himself to go into another room to get something. When he came back, he brought his Bible. He continued talking, "I read something just a few days ago I want to show you." Alvin found what he was looking for in short order.

"Ah! Here it is!" He showed the two men. They got noticeably irritated by what they read.

"That is the old writings," one fellow said. "We have a better understanding now."

"I thought you said your new plan was taken from ancient writings."

"It was after this!" pointing to Alvin's Bible.

"Wasn't Isaiah a true prophet of God?"

"Yes, but this is a bad interpretation."

"And yours is better?"

"Oh yes, much better."

"I must ask you to go now," Alvin said as he stood from his chair. "Your message is not welcome here."

"But, but---," one sputtered, "Please read this book and we will come back and talk some more."

"No. Take your book with you, and don't come back until you know the truth." The two left. Alice was speechless for awhile, then she asked Alvin about his attitude.

Alvin explained: "Isaiah 43:10 and 11 says, 'Ye are my witnesses, saith the Lord, and my servant whom I have chosen; that ye may know and believe me, and understand that I am He: Before me there was no God formed, neither shall there be after me. I, even I, am the Lord; and beside me there is no Savior'." Alice then understood. It must be true, the religion of those guys was not Christian.

Mr. Rush called Ben the next day, telling him about the conversation with the fellows that had come calling. "Did I do right?" he asked Ben.

Ben encouraged him by saying, "For not knowing

much about their religion, you did all you could do. Do you think they might return?"

"I doubt it. I told them to take their book and not come back. I didn't feel good doing it, but what choice did I have?"

"Pastor McKenzie knows a lot about them (the religion). What do you suppose would be the chances of them listening to the truth?"

Alvin thought about that for a moment. "It would have to involve someone other than me. There is a small possibility they would return if I called and apologized for my attitude. I really am reluctant to let them back in my house."

"You do know how to contact them then?"

"Their card is in my trash. Hold on. I'll see if I can find it." Alvin looked and was successful. "I found it." He read the phone number and names to Ben. Ben copied the information.

"I won't try this without Mark's help. I will call you, whether we do or don't OK?"

****

Mark and Ben were given permission to use a small party room in a local café for one evening since nobody with a group of any size needed to use it that particular evening. Alvin made the call to Tim, one of the two that had visited him at his home.

"Two of my friends are willing to talk to you. They are probably more curious than I was. I will be there to introduce them to you and you to them. Personally, I am still of the same persuasion and intend to remain there." The fellow said that he understood. Alvin called Ben. Ben called Mark. The time and date was still all right with each of them. That Sunday, Mark gave Ben and Alvin a quick lesson in the religion of Alvin's callers, then prayed that God would be present at the small meeting. The ladies' prayer circle promised to be praying during the café meeting. They had seen several occasions that prayer was answered when they (the ladies) had prayed during a certain situation. The first time was during the apprehension of the cult at the cliffs.

The evening came for the meeting. One of the guests arrived on time. The second man was to arrive soon. When it became apparent that the other man would be late, Mark suggested that they go ahead and order their meals. Religion was not discussed during the meal. By the time the men had finished their meals, it appeared that the second man was not going to attend.

Ben asked the one guest, "Would it be all right if we just talk even without Tim? We didn't intend to make it a three-against-two game anyway. And now even more so, not three against one." Martin agreed. He seemed to be increasingly at ease.

Ben began this way: "I am Ben Reed. My occupation is to care for a forest reserve. I am known as The Ranger. Becky is my wife, and Daniel my son. In no way do I worship the plants and animals, but I do often point toward God who created it all. Should I be required to not mention God in my vocation, then I must have the wrong vocation. Alvin you have already met. Mark is this community's pastor. We are honored to learn from him and work with him. He is not our king, but a brother in the Lord. Mark!"

Mark told about his wife, son and daughter. He too welcomed Martin, "I brought my Bible, but not my gun, and I am not a cannibal or a vampire."

Martin understood that he was among friends, and he expressed that he was feeling more comfortable as the evening progressed. "We nearly always go out in pairs, but I won't just eat and run. I only have one wife and to this point four children. My parents raised me in the religion I am in at the present. My wife was also, so.........what I am saying is, I know my religion much better than I do yours. I suppose as a way to start, I will try to answer questions. Tim usually did this part."

Mark broke what could have become an awkward silence. He stealthily approached it by making a statement: "Martin, I celebrate Christmas, not because that was when God was born, but that was when we celebrate God becoming a man. The Bible explains it as, 'When the time was right....' God had told the very first woman that this would come. Jesus was born of woman but was the Son of God, and also God the Son. He came to seek and to save that which was lost. I am one of those he came to seek and save. Do you share this knowledge?"

Martin smiled bravely, "Sure! We say it a bit differently, but it is similar."

Mark wanted to hear, "How do you say it?"

Martin wished Tim was here, He suppressed the

urge to roll his eyes. "Jesus is the Savior of the world. He was found to be perfect. What he did was accepted by his God who appointed him to be our God."

Ben felt he needed to ask: "He was accepted by God because He was perfect?"

"There was never recorded anything evil about Jesus. If there were, God saw to it that it was erased." Martin added. Mark had studied about their religion, but somehow it felt more shocking when he heard it personally from one of them.

"That would leave it open for anyone to be chosen to be God......if he were good enough."

Alvin didn't expect to enter any of the conversation, but the timing was perfect for him to ask, "Remember the scripture I showed you at my house? Gods don't just come and go at the whim of other gods!"

"We have better evidence than.....the old writings of your Bible."

Mark was afraid that anger could erupt and escalate. "Martin, let me show you another scripture, to illustrate what we believe. It is not ancient. It was written about twenty to thirty years after Jesus walked this earth as a man. Here it is." Mark turned his Bible so Martin could read. Ephesians two, verses eight and nine were underlined. Martin read it and looked up, first at Mark, then in turn, at Ben and Alvin. "I have never seen this before. Don't you guys believe you get rewards for living a good life?"

"Yes, we do."

"Then why are we at loggerheads?"

Mark turned the Bible back so he could read, starting where Martin had left off, "For we are His workmanship, created in Christ Jesus unto good works, which God hath before ordained that we should walk in them. Verse thirteen: But now in Christ Jesus ye who sometimes were far off are made nigh by the blood of Christ. For He is our peace." Mark stopped reading and began quoting from memory: "For God so loved the world that He gave His only begotten Son that whosoever believeth in Him should not perish, but have everlasting life. God has given us eternal life. This life is in His Son. Whosoever has the Son has life; whosoever has not the Son of God, has not life. Behold, I stand at the door and knock. If any man hear my voice and open the door, I will come in and sup with him and he with me." Mark turned to Ben. "Ben do you believe Jesus died for your sins and by his death and resurrection has secured for you eternal life?"

"I surely do! With all my heart!"

"Alvin, do you have this hope?"

"Ever since the fire, yes. I remember that night!"

"Martin, is Jesus your personal Savior? Do you know in your heart He gave His life for you?"

"I want to believe that......that He accepts me. Would I need to join your church? Would I need to renounce all I have been taught?"

Mark felt his heart go out to Martin, "Martin, everyone who comes to God must believe that He is, and that He rewards them who diligently seek Him. Yet no one can come to God unless God first draw him. May I pray that you feel God drawing you to himself through His

Son Jesus Christ? And what Church you join is between you and God. The only thing you need to renounce is what is not truth. God will teach you that also."

"Yes. That would be fine."

Mark asked Ben and Alvin to touch Martin's arm or hand as he prayed. Resting a hand on Martin's shoulder as he sat beside him. Mark reached out to God on Martin's behalf. All four men were shedding tears as they felt the Holy Spirit enter the room and probably on each of them.

As Mark said "Amen," Martin asked, "What do I do now?"

"In your own words, thank God that He loves you this much, and has saved you for eternity."

"Thank you Jesus!" Martin prayed. "Thank you Jesus!"

Just then another person entered the room. He saw the tear-streaked faces of the four men and stopped dead in his tracks. Martin jumped to his feet and took Tim's hand, leading him to the other three. "I am in, Tim! I am saved!"

"You didn't!"

"I did, and He can save you too!"

"Martin," Tim said. "Get a hold of yourself! We came to get them, not the other way around!"

"They never got me!"

"Good!"

"God did!" finishing what he was saying.

Tim muttered something about car problems and about, if only he had been here. "Get over it!" he said, and left.

"You may get a lot of that," Mark told Martin. Jesus said, 'In this world you will have tribulation, but be of good cheer, I have overcome the world.' Be prepared to meet lots of discouragement. Go easy on those who don't know, yet."

"Like my wife and children?"

"Especially them."

"I will, thanks. I would pay for my dinner!"

"No way." Ben said, "Maybe the next time. Later on down the road, we can include your family."

"I would like that, and I pray they will too, by then. May we meet your wife and baby, if we get together?"

"For sure! Let's exchange addresses." They proceeded to do that.

Mark told Martin, "You are likely to have doubts about all you heard and learned this evening. Consider this: We don't gain points or get any favors for helping you reach out to understand God better. If you noticed, we did not bad-mouth your old religion, and we won't.

Neither did we introduce you to some new and better plan. The Bible still says the same things it did when it was first written. It wasn't revised each time someone had a better idea. You found the only way to escape the penalty for sin by accepting the one who died in your place. Might I suggest that each time you doubt, you either read this verse and do what it says, or after you have learned it, obey it." Mark handed Martin a napkin with the book, chapter and verse number written on it. Martin looked at it and put it in his jacket pocket. He then turned to Alvin.

"My friend, you were right. Your relationship with God is better than my old religion which was not welcome at your home. Thank you for calling me to return." Alvin nodded and smiled.

Martin left his old book on the café table. "I won't need that." He then left.

Ben called Becky. "Coming home; prayers answered." Becky called the prayer chain.

Chapter eight
Coloring Books

It had been some time since they had gotten together and talked, Becky reminded herself as she brought her car to a stop at Steve and Sharon's house. Sharon was expecting her. Since parenting takes time, and winter weather hinders travel, both could have been used as excuses for their delayed woman-to-woman talks. Becky hoped the reason wasn't the fact that she had had her first child before Sharon had.

Becky carefully took Daniel from his car seat without waking him. Carrying him against her shoulder with one arm, she took the diaper bag with the other hand and closed the car door. Sharon was holding little Grace as she stood at her open door inviting Becky inside.

"Ah, he's asleep."

"The long ride did it to him. He'll wake up shortly." Sharon started fixing a place on the divan for Becky to lay Daniel.

"The floor is fine. If it were cold, it would be different." She laid him on his blanket. Grace was taking notice that she was not the only little one in the room She was still so young that it was hard to imagine what she was thinking. At least she could hold her head up and look his direction as she lay on her tummy just out of reach. Her little hands were moving as if she was wanting to touch. She was not yet in the crawling stage, so touching Daniel was not in her capability.

"Daniel has really grown! What can he do?"

"He crawls and wants to stand. Of course Ben holds him in the standing position about every evening lately. Daniel just loves it. He is highly curious, wanting to inspect everything at his level."

"What does Grace weigh now? You know, this is the first I have seen her since the day after she was born."

"Is that true?"

"Yes. We have missing you in church."

"We have been attending my parent's church, when we go. It is closer, you know. Oh, fourteen pounds. Daniel?"

"Eighteen, and a gigantic appetite." About then Daniel stirred, starting to awaken. "See, we talk about food, and he wakes up."

"Are you still breast feeding?"

"Yes, but I can't feed him peas, beets, and applesauce that way; and pudding. He likes his pudding. You?"

"Some, but I am about ready to go to formula all the time. Formula is a lot easier in public Do you, in public?"

"That is usually water bottle time. Hi, little man!" Becky greeted as Daniel's eyes came open to see a different setting. "You had a nice nap." Daniel grinned, then seeing Sharon and little Grace, he reached his arms up to Mama. She lifted him to her lap.

Sharon was observing, and apparently still wanting to learn. "You picked him up as soon as he woke up. Is that..?"

"Spoiling him? No. We call it maintaining security. Letting him get scared or frustrated before we act is never good. Independence will come soon enough, but to force it is not good at this age. I have seen other people's problems develop when they appear to be bothered when their child wants security up close."

"How about getting them to go to sleep?"

"That is easier too, when the TV goes down or off, and they know they won't be forsaken when they wake up. Ben and I both rise early, which also helps calm a child to easily get to sleep at night."

"I sleep as late as I can," Sharon stated. "Sometimes Grace's crying is what wakes me." Becky was wise to withhold comment. "The psychologists say things like that won't hurt a child."

"How many of them have happy healthy trusting babies; and children of any age?" Sharon looked as if she was trying to find words to say, or a question to ask. When she didn't right away, Becky continued. "This is our love. Children can and do sense it. They need never to feel like orphans."

"When they grow into coloring books, we are to reinforce them by bragging about their coloring, right?"

"At least acknowledge their efforts, and whenever possible, color a page alongside them so they will see how to improve their own techniques."

"Adults....coloring?"

"An example shown is better than an admonishment for poor effort."

"How many children have you had? You seem too wise to be on your first one."

"My mother was my example. She even taught me how to give a simple kiss."

"I taught Steve how to kiss," Sharon quickly said, without thinking how it sounded.

"Yes, that kind you either learn together or else one of you had a previous teacher." Sharon appeared to regret her statement of her kissing expertise. Becky added a little more. "The trouble with those previous teachers is that they usually want more than kisses. Mama warned me about those."

"My mother didn't tell me anything, and I was their only child."

"Did she color in your book or show you how to sew on a button?"

"No. She knew I would learn on my own, I guess."

"Just think now; what was the result of teaching Steve how to kiss? Wasn't it the forerunner of your fear of a pregnancy?"

"Well, I was not sure he would ever kiss me that way, had I not shown him. I wouldn't be surprised if that wasn't part of the reason his first marriage crumbled so quickly."

"You were his first experience while he was not yours."

"Something like that."

"He probably will never ask or even want to know, but Steve may be haunted by the thoughts of what else your teachers taught you."

"Why might he think about that?"

"Because of your sexy kisses and other indications that would signal that he was not your first."

"I would not want him to think that."

"Did you tell him that he was your first?"

"I don't remember. Don't tell him, if you think otherwise…….please!"

"That's not my job."

"It's mine?"

"No. Don't lie if he asks, but don't fill in any details if he does. When Steve reaches for you, pick him up, so to speak, and hold him."

"And if he is too proud to reach?"

"Then keep reaching for him until he becomes trusting enough to reach to you. Otherwise he may be experiencing that orphan syndrome."

"He is a grown man!"

"Yes, and talking to Bessie may be his only solace."

"Bessie?"

"Isn't that his mare's name?"

"I guess so."

"Offer to color a page in his book with him."

"Brush down a horse with him; I get it now!"

"I found I needed to wean off my computer somewhat, to be a better wife."

"Ouch! I didn't want to hear that, but it is probably true for me too."

"Before I reveal too many of my flaws, I had better go cook my little family some supper. Thanks for the visit. You know where we live."

"Yeah, this was good. Looks like Grace and Daniel are enjoying their visit also." Sharon and Becky hugged. "Go get out your crayons." They both laughed. The two ladies promised to visit more often, and not just by telephone or computer.

Becky got Daniel loaded for travel, and headed back to tree country.

Chapter nine
Dry, Very Dry

Several miles on the other side of town from the forest acres was farming country. How long would that last? It had been a long time since measurable rain had fallen. At the end of an awfully hot day, several of the farmers and ranchers came together at a country chapel.

"My corn is curling because of the drought," one said.

"My chickens have nearly stopped laying and our milk cow dried up," another stated. "Since my wheat crop was not that good and the price even worse, I may have to sell out."

"Me too," said Lawrence. He was a man of few words, but he said it all by those few.

The pastor of the church let all who wanted to speak, have their say, then he asked, "So then, would you agree that what we need is a good soaking rain?"

At first they all just looked at him as if waiting to hear something intelligent.

"The weatherman hasn't seen any on the horizon for at least the next two weeks," Ron pointed out.

"That will be two weeks too late for me," Jeb lamented.

"Then we had better order some," the pastor said.

"We have all been prayin' fer rain," Lawrence said. "You know we have."

"Do you believe your prayers were answered?"

"Taint rainin' none," Lawrence said. It was obvious. There was not a day that someone had not prayed for rain, but the rain was seeming to be less likely.

"Then let's open the word and see what God says about this." Some of the guys took the Bibles from the song book rack on the back of the pews. They waited for a clue on where to turn.

"Romans eight, verse twenty-eight. Let's start there." The pastor waited until everyone found the spot, then proceeded. "What does it say, Bill?"

"It says…I don't get it! How could a drought be good?"

"Are you sure we have the right scripture?" Jeb asked.

"OK, let's try another one. Turn to First Thessalonians five, verses sixteen through eighteen." Once again, he waited until they found the passage.

"This makes less sense than the other one," Ron commented. "I'm going home!"

"Wait a minute, Ron," Mike said. "The pastor's right. It's all about faith, right Pastor?"

"Absolutely right, Mike. Ya got any?"

"By George, I do! Could I lead a prayer?"

"Go for it!" the pastor said. Those who were about to leave, stopped beside the pews they had gotten up from. They were raised better than to be moving about during a prayer.

Mike closed his eyes, "Father, I am so sorry for the way I have been so ungrateful. You know best and always give us what we need. When you see that we need it, you give us the faith to ask for it. We see evidence that we need rain. We don't suppose that you are blind. Anyway, thank you for your care for us even though our faith is so small. And Lord, when you see fit, thank you for the rain. Thank you for the crop-saving rain. Amen."

"Amen," said the pastor. He was the only one who echoed Mike's amen.

The afternoon had become the darkening evening. It appeared that cars were driving by, shining their lights on the chapel windows. Strange though, usually the car motors could be heard. There were no outside noises; strange, really strange.

The pastor started to smile, "Mike, He is answering!"

"Lightning?" Mike asked. "There was only one little cloud when we got here."

"Open the doors, Ron or Lawrence." They did, preparing to leave. Ron stepped back, bumping into Lawrence, because of what he saw. Lawrence saw it too, gasped then fell on his knees. Bill and Ron both hit the floor unashamedly. The distant lightning could be seen and the thunder could barely be heard; each succeeding clap getting a bit louder. Speechless, the guys waited in awe, and with increasing hope, watched. At this point, time didn't seem to matter and no one complained that their knees hurt on the hardwood floor. After a long period of waiting and watching, big drops started to fall. Not much more time passed before the surface of the ground was entirely wet.

"Praise the Lord!" Mike yelled, and he ran out into what would soon be a downpour. "Praise the Lord!" One man's faith, in a sea of much doubt and drought, seemed to be enough. Yes, it would be enough. Rain! Much rain. Much God-given rain. Always enough, never too late, for those with real faith.

"I hope it is raining on the unjust too," Ron said ashamedly. "God forgive me!"

"Me too!" Lawrence said, still a man of few words.

Chapter ten
Halloween? No!

"It's a what?" Ben asked, when Mark called.

"A locally produced Biblical drama." Mark said again. The cast is made up from local folks and put on for three or four evenings."

"Is it a shock drama, like a spook house?"

"Not Halloween, if that is what you are thinking," Mark said. "Our family went to see one last night and I got infected,"

"Infected," Ben said, not so much a question.

"Will I guess there is probably a better word, but I can't seem to think of it right now."

"You got enamored with the possibility of doing it here."

"Yeah! That's the word! Melinda, Nick, and I saw it, and we are sure that if enough people can be encouraged to make up the cast, we can swing it in our community. We may have to start small the first year."

"As what, a fund raiser?"

"No! As an evangelistic/revival aid. May we show you what we have in mind?"

"Sure! Becky is out visiting, or on her way home. We will probably have supper over by 8:00. Would an hour be enough time to explain it?"

"That is plenty of time to outline the plan."

"I will call you back when Beck gets home and she is willing to listen tonight. I see lights coming up the driveway now; must be her."

Ben went out and carried Daniel to the house. He asked Becky if she would mind if the McKenzies visited after supper.

"Great! It has never been just them and us." It was true. Usually there were several more in their get-togethers, and a Bible study was the reason for the occasion. Ben made the call, then asked Becky about her day. Becky gave him the abbreviated version of her visit with Sharon. She would tell him more later, when they didn't have the upcoming visit pending. Ben did the same with what he had been told by Mark. A little was all he knew anyway.

The McKenzies arrived just before 8:00. Their daughter came with them. She volunteered to play with Daniel while the adults talked. Nick stayed home, doing some school research on the computer.

"What do you have?" Ben asked, when the four were comfortably seated.

"The title," Mark told them, "And that is subject to change. What we saw was arranged this way: Scenes were set up with the story progressing toward a climax or climaxes. A number of folk, led by a tour guide, if you will, go through the sequence of scenes until they reach the end. At that time they are challenged to condense what they saw and how it may or may not relate to themselves. The personal climax that each would reach would depend on their situation and type of burden each carried."

"And their burden," Becky surmised, "Could be their own private life, sinful or otherwise."

"Right on!" Mark said, as he pointed a finger toward her. "The story line could be simple, or it could be much more complex. As you may have guessed, we don't have a story yet."

Ben looked at Becky then Melinda, and finally at Mark, who was looking at him. "What is our part?"

"We need a story to tell. You did really good for the school children, and you both wrote a great account of Ben's mountain adventure. By the time we had put together the resurrection pageant, people knew of your abilities to put something great together."

"You two had as much input on that as we did," Becky said.

"Could you?" Mark asked, looking at both Ben and Becky.

"Wow!" Becky said humbly. The task would be big. "We would need to know the layout of what you saw, and how many scenes are needed to tell the story. I am willing. How about you, Ben?"

"No promises on how soon we will have it finished, but sure, if you promise to veto the result, if our efforts don't meet the requirements."

"I know that won't be necessary, even before you start. What we saw had ten scenes. There were a few sound effects, but mostly acting. Each scene took from four to six minutes to perform. Group movements, coupled with tour guide announcements, took several minutes between each scene. The final stop as a group would be in a room with a Christian pastor, who would, while quickly summarizing the story, challenge the individuals in the group to apply the outcome of the story to their individual lives. Those wanting to trust the Lord for the first time, or wanting prayer for self, friends or family will be led by a counselor to a private spot for that purpose."

"That might require several counselors,," Ben supposed.

"Yes, it could. They would have to be chosen very carefully."

"Becky, if you have nothing on your calendar for Saturday," Ben suggested, "Let's spend the day in prayer and see what the Lord gives us."

"I am open," Becky said. "And already I have an idea for part of it."

"You two may be done in that one day," Melinda said, bragging on them.

"The Schwartz's have sound equipment and can make situation recordings, such as helicopter sounds, sirens, and things like that," Mark offered. He filled them in on the possibility of renting a finished drama if no local drama could be made. "Again I have full confidence in you two."

"Is there one that Becky and I can go see, to get a format to build on?"

"Melinda, doesn't the one we saw run through tomorrow?"

"Yes it does. Tomorrow is its third and final night. We can watch Daniel if you want to go." It was a big hour's drive away. They would go.

The next morning, Becky called the number Mark had given them. They got a 7:15 P.M. reservation. The earlier times were already filled.

****

The story line was one that used wrecked cars and a loud helicopter sound effect. Ben and Becky could hear it as they parked their car a half block away. "Sounds real," Ben said. They entered the building and was directed to the lady with the reservation information. After confirming that their reservation was still the same, they joined the group that was forming. While they were waiting, they could hear what sounded like a horror movie being played in an adjoining room. Could that be part of this drama?

"Group five, take your seats behind the blue curtain," the tour guide announced. The Reeds joined the group at 7:18. The guide introduced the drama and bade the fourteen people to follow her. Gathering near her at a door marked, "Scene One," the guide knocked once on the door then announced clues as to who would be seen behind the door.

After her small speech, she knocked twice and opened the door while saying, "Follow me and stay behind the blue line."

When all fifteen were in the room, the door was shut and latched. Scene one came to life. It was a fast-moving scene. (The main characters, that would be played by other folks in later scenes, were introduced as part of the story by the common dress code for each character, so the audience could identify them later.)

Scene two was enacted in the same manner as scene one. Scenes three through five continued the plot. Scene six had the wrecked cars and the helicopter sound. Scene seven was a dying scene. Scene eight was a judgment scene, and scene nine the hell scene, which did indeed use the horrible sounds heard earlier. Scene ten was a thing of beauty: Heaven was decked in white and gold throughout, and was occupied by angels. There was a figure sitting on a throne. Yes! It was Him! (not really) He welcomed the group, one at a time, to Heaven, and thanked them for coming.

The group was then led to a room of chairs, where they sat. How would the audience apply the drama to their own lives? They had that opportunity. Counselors were there for individuals, to guide them to any decision they wanted to make. Ben and Becky had made their decision to give it their best effort to the making of a similar drama for their town and community.

Chapter eleven
The Plan Comes Together

Ben and Becky did work on their drama ideas on Saturday, just after they had seen the drama the evening before. "Scene one should be a dysfunctional couple or family," Becky suggested

"Yes, and scene two would be some sort of separation because of the dysfunction. An emotional separation would work well here," Ben proposed. Becky agreed.

"Scene three could be mistakes made, or temptations to make them, because of the separation. Does that seem proper at this point?" Ben asked.

"I'll write it down even if we have to place it in some other scene to make it fit. Scene four could be a crisis which could force a separation not caused by either of the couple."

Ben was curious as to what Becky had in mind to fill that bill. Now it was his turn to plan a scene. "Scene five is a stalemated recovery, but a partial recovery none-the-less."

"Got it!" Becky said as she wrote it down.

"Scene six is a disaster averted just in time by a friend," Ben said matter-of-factly. They both knew what that scene was about.

"Ben, couldn't scene seven be years later-------a judgment for three or more?"

"OK, and we had better get the hell scene in next, and make scene nine the Heaven scene."

"Don't you think we ought to get their permission before we get close to their real life?" Becky asked. Ben agreed. He was pretty sure that what he had in mind for scene two or three was not from their real life anyway. Could they change scene four to make it any more dramatic than it truly was? Probably not. The once dysfunctional couple was called and then visited.

"You two are the only ones who know our real story, right?" the husband asked.

"I never told anyone," Ben assured the man.

"And what went on between you and me in your house that afternoon," Becky told his wife, "I never leaked to a soul, other than Ben."

The man looked at his wife and asked, "Wouldn't you say it was for a good cause, providing the names are changed?"

The wife answered by asking Ben and Becky, "May we see the whole plan before we give full permission? And if the ending is wrong, our permission is off."

It was the only way the Reeds would do it anyway. It was quite fair. These couples had become close friends in the last year. Nothing should be told to destroy that. Ben prayed for God's guidance, and each one hugged each of the other couple.

"I love you, Mary Lou," the man said to his wife (not her real name).

"I love you too, Lazarus," she said, and gave him a hug.

"God bless you two!" Becky told them. It was obvious that God had done just that.

Ben felt he should say more. "We are likely to make parts of the drama to only slightly resemble the actual events in your lives. So in advance, forgive us if you are disappointed in the outcome. Some of the things we know, that you shared with us in confidence, or your emotions, won't be compromised just to make a drama. It might not even be recognizable to you." They were understanding, and more-so, obviously very relieved.

****

The drama script was approved. Five evenings will be chosen later for the rehearsals and the actual drama. Lots of calls would be made, and advertising would cover towns and cities within a hundred mile radius. If the desire to see it were as infectious as the desire to participate, all three nights of the performance would be busy.

"I was just figuring," Becky told Ben one Sunday evening, "We could be doing this thing nearly fifty times in three evenings! Fifty times fifteen would be.......seven hundred fifty people! Could that be right?"

"I wouldn't doubt it."

"Build it and they will come," Becky said. "God will bring them. I heard something like that somewhere." Ben knew what she was referring to.

The weeks ahead were busy for many of the church people. Although the script was accepted by the unnamed couple, they asked to not be chosen to act in it, since it was much too close for comfort. "We would like to see it though," the husband said. "Couldn't we do that?" he asked his wife. She was slightly uncomfortable, but nodded yes.

Clothing, scenery, food for the actors, drama site, hours of operation chosen, prayer times, and suggested offerings to recover the costs were some of the things that had to be considered and decided. Mark and Melinda prayed that it not fizzle and flop, and the weather would cooperate.

"That is up to you, Lord," Mark prayed aloud.

Volunteers came out of the woodwork. Ladies from another church in a neighboring town would bring the food for the actors all three nights. Another church, which had a super color copier would make the posters. School children volunteered to spread the posters around the local community. Newspaper and radio ads would be a big part also. Posters were sent to churches in other communities, along with permission for duplication as needed in those places.

"Ben!" Becky exclaimed, "This is getting to be larger than us!"

"But not larger than God," Ben reminded her. Becky knew that, which helped the moment of anxiety to subside.

Poor Melinda. She has the phone that all the reservation requests would be called to. "Other people will assume that responsibility once the drama is in full swing," Melinda tried to assure Becky. "Don't worry. It will work out. My two children are old enough to understand. Yours aren't. You have done your part by writing it. How did you do that?"

"We did good with Ben's lost and found story, so I guess it came natural to write this."

Chapter twelve
Adult Drama

About half of the reservations for the first night had been assigned by the time that evening's performance started. Stragglers would fill in other available times, it was supposed. Each of the second and third performances would fill, hopefully, as needed.

At the first and second rehearsals, the actors of the scenes got to go through the whole drama so they could see it also. And who would have guessed; eight actors gave their lives to the Lord, by faith, after seeing the rehearsal.

On the first evening of the performance, the actors gathered in the sanctuary for a time of praise, worship and prayer. After the encouragement, they straggled to the fellowship hall for a small meal. The actual performance was next. Even though they had written the script and also the tour guide lines, Ben and Becky were thrilled to be in the first group to see the entire drama. The cast was, in part, over full in that there were some understudies. To give all their chance, they sometimes alternated, taking every other performance filling that character.

Seated in group one, the Reeds listened to the words they had written, now being read back to the group by the tour guide, along with some more information.

Guide: "This drama was written by someone who could be our neighbors. Only a few know who they are. I do not know, and it is not necessary to know. The story line for this drama could be happening today. It may be that parts if it has happened in your home. Follow me to scene one and form a semi-circle around me as I introduce the scene to you. No talking please, and turn off all cell phones now. OK, follow me. They did. At the door of the first scene, the semi-circle was formed as instructed. The guide knocked once on the scene-one door, then began talking.

Guide: "Behind this door we will find a couple, married yet so different; he a believer and she, not so much. Stay on this side of the blue line on the floor when we enter, so they will have room to do their parts." The guide made two knocks on the door then entered, leading her group.

There sat a lady with one leg tucked under the other and a big book in her lap. The guide closed the door. Enter one man, tying his tie as he enters.

Jim: "I take it I am going to church alone again today," he states.

Pat: "You know I have to cram for my A & P test. I can do that better without interruptions."

Jim: "See ya." He heads for the door, "I wouldn't

know a triceps or a bicuspid from a corpuscle. Hope you do."

Pat: "Umm," she mutters something about him being a dummy as he exits and closes the door.

A car motor is heard starting and is heard accelerating as the sound fades. The lady closes her book, goes to get a bag of chips, and returns to sit at a computer, starting it, bringing up a game.

The guide opens the door. Her group follows her to another door and gathers close.

Guide: "In this scene, Jim is doing his trucking business; sometimes coming home in the middle of the week, sometimes not. Follow me."

Pat: (phone rings) "H'lo?" She listens. "Hi, Ellen...you saw what?... Wouldn't surprise me...No, I didn't know...He'll pay for it, big time." (She hangs up the phone, pauses, then calls her mother). "Mom, may I come over? My gall bladder is on the rampage. I will be closer to my doctor there. Jim is at work...No, he doesn't know, and wouldn't care...I just know, that's all." She slowly gets up while holding her tummy. To herself she mutters, "So he's got another woman does he? Not for long!" Pat gets her purse after putting a bottle of pills into it. She aims her keys toward a window. A car is heard starting. She writes a note and places it on a table.

Guide, at scene three: "Pat thinks Jim is seeing another woman. Ellen, who likes to be a know-it-all, and who works at a truck stop, saw something, which she passed on to Pat. Let's see what she saw."

A cardboard or similar lightweight board is cut out like a small version of a semi cab with sleeper, trailer not in sight. When the tour group is in place, and the door closed: A slender woman comes into the room from stage right. She goes behind the truck cab, and is seen entering from behind. She goes into the sleeper.

Almost immediately, Jim comes from the same direction with his brown bag lunch in hand, which he had purchased at the truck stop. He opens the truck door and gets in the driver's seat. He closes the door. He starts the truck (recorded truck sounds) accelerates, shifts gears until he has reached high gear; the woman speaks from the sleeper.

Woman: "Hi, Jimmy!"

Jim: "What? Who's there?" he turns his head to his right, looking toward the sleeper. The woman appears coming up beside him.

Woman: "It is me! Surprised?"

Jim: "What are you doing? You shouldn't be in here!"

Woman: "You need some company. I will bet you don't get my kind at home. Stop somewhere and come back when you are ready." (woman goes back into the sleeper) (the truck motor is heard decelerating, accelerating again, decelerating, pulling to a stop, air brakes applied)

Woman: "We're stopping?" the woman asks gleefully.

Jim: "I need to unload."

Woman: "I didn't know you had a load."

Jim: "You need to get out!"

Woman: (looks out of the sleeper) "We are back at the truck stop!"

Jim: "Out!"

Woman: "You are going to miss me!" She gets out of the back side of the cab and walks past the front of the truck. Another man walks onto the stage. She takes his arm. "Let me see your truck!" They exit toward right stage. He is smiling.

Young man: "Yes ma'am!" that scene ends.

Guide at door four: "This is a hospital. A doctor is talking to Pat's mother."

Doctor: "Your daughter is lucky to be alive. She not only had a ruptured gall bladder, but also peritonitis. Recovery will take a long time, if in fact she does recover. She is in intensive care in an induced coma. We should call her husband."

Evelyn: "I will do it." She calls

Jim: "Evelyn! I saw Pat's note."

Evelyn: "Jim, she is in the hospital; may not make it. Can you come?"

Jim: "I will make it happen. First, I need to cancel today's job." The conversation ends and Jim dials his phone. "Al, Jim, you know how I told you about Pat and me? …our problems….She's in the hospital, may not make it. I need to go."

Al: "Didn't you say that you had some loads to take today?"

Jim: "I will have to cancel."

Al: "Tell me where they are, and the times, and I will run them for you."

Jim: "Ever run a beef taxi?"

Al: "Drove semis in the army. Start her up and leave me load instructions. You just go!"

Jim: "Thanks, I'll do it." (scene ends)

Guide at scene at scene five: We go to the Hospital where Jim talks to Evelyn, Pat's mom.

Jim: "You go home and get some rest. I will call you if there is any change."

Evelyn: "Thanks, Jim."

The doctor enters the waiting room after Evelyn leaves

Doctor: "She is lightly sedated. She might be able to talk. Want to see her?"

Jim: "Sure do!" He goes to Pat's bedside.

Pat: "Zim?"

Jim: "Hi Pat. I am here."

Pat: "Whad I get in 'natomy?"

Jim: "Got a C plus. Congratulations!"

Pat: "Nod workin' today?"

Jim: "Al's finishing my week for me."

Pat: "So sleepy."

Jim: "Get some rest." She sleeps.

Nurse: "Pat is taking A & P?"

Jim: "Bombed the first try. Had to drop out. Couldn't tell her. She doesn't remember."

Nurse: "You're a good husband."

Jim: "Thanks."

Scene six Guide: "Pat slowly recovered physically and got to go home. Al's wife Betty feels she ought to call on her. She tells Al and goes. Jim is out trucking again. We are at Jim and Pat's house.

(Betty knocks on Pat's door. Pat opens it a little)

Betty: "I am Al's wife, Betty. I think I am suppose to visit with you."

Pat: Hesitates, then slowly opens the door wider. "Well, come in then." Pat shuts door after Betty enters. "You guys and your God! What enchanted thing did he tell you to tell me?"

Betty: "He wants me to tell you He loves you. How are you doin…really?"

Pat: "You don't want to know."

Betty: "Why not?"

Pat: "Because you are so blessed……..and I am so at the bottom of nowhere."

Betty: "Then that is probably why I was sent here."

Pat: "To rub my face in it?"

Betty: "No, to tell you God has a wonderful plan for your life."

Pat: "Then why haven't I read it?"

Betty: "I don't know. It's there."

Pat leaves the room, brings back a very dusty Bible and tosses it on the coffee table.

Pat: "Show me! There is no Patricia in there anywhere."

Betty opens the dusty Bible and turns a few pages.

Betty: "Here it is." She hands the Bible to Pat while pointing to John 3;16. Pat reads. "Couldn't the word, whosoever, be easily replaced with Pat, to read: If Pat believes in Him, she will not perish, but have everlasting life?" (she turns to John 1;12) "As Pat receives Him, to her gave He power to become a daughter of God."

Pat: After Betty finds another verse, Pat reads aloud: "God hath given unto us eternal life; this life is in his Son. He who hath the Son hath life; He who hath not the Son of God, hath not life."

Betty: "In this world you will have tribulation, but be of good cheer, I have overcome the world. Jesus even prayed for you and me." Betty finds John 17 and hands it to Pat. She reads silently for a little while.

Pat: How do we get on His good side?"

Betty: finding Revelation 3;20: "Behold I stand at the door and knock. If any man (or woman) should hear my voice and open the door, I will come in and sup with him and he with me."

Pat: "How do we get to where He is?" Betty finds John 14: 6. Pat reads, "I am the way, the truth and the life. No man comes unto the Father but by me." She ponders the words she just read. "Come here a minute." Pat leads Betty to her kitchen where many containers of medicine are on the table. "I was getting ready to take them all, or until I passed out, or died."

Betty: "Let's go back in here." They go back into the living room. "May I pray for you?"

Pat: "Please!"

Betty: adlibs a prayer for Pat then finishes by praying, "Pat can only come to you if you invite her to come. I pray that you are calling her now and she hears your voice."

Pat: (tearfully) "Thank you Jesus, for your invitation, and for sending Betty to show the way to trust in you." (can ad lib more as the group is leaving)

At scene seven, Guide: "Several years later, some have died. Was it from a car bomb? No. Was it old age or disease? Yes. This might be the stories of some of the people that we have seen in the previous scenes."

(At Hell, scene seven)

Demon 1: "Here comes our master!"

Satan: (booming voice) "Who have you brought while I was gone?"

Demon 2: "A trucker and a woman."

Satan: (booming) "A man and his wife?"

Demon 2: "No, just two ordinary people."

Satan: (booming) "Why did we get them?"

Demon 1: "We don't know. They were having fun in a truck before they got sick."

Satan: (booming) "Bring them to me." (trucker and rider enter) "Why are you here?"

Man: "Disease got us. I guess we gave it to each other."

Woman: "How could we have known? Why are we at this place?"

Satan (booming) "You have been told why you are here; sin!"

Woman: "Was it so wrong?"

Man to the woman: "We have had lots of sin."

Satan (booming): "Join the others in torment."

Man and woman: "No! This is too much! No!" (the two are led behind a black curtain by darkened creatures;

they are still screaming)

Satan: (to the crowd of watchers; booming) "Will I be seeing some of you next? Get out of here!" (door opens and watchers hurriedly leave)

Guide at scene eight: "This is our final scene. One more stop remains after this. You may need to make some choices, if you have not already. A proper covering will be given to you before you enter. Enter reverently and stay on the golden path." (a white towel is placed on the shoulders around the neck of each in the group, before they enter the beautiful white and gold adorned room) Ben and Becky were still among the first group as they gathered on the golden cross path.

Gate keeper: "We have three more!"

Person on the throne: "Ah, Al and Betty and Pat. Welcome to Heaven!"

Pat: "Why am I here? I have been so bad. Jim has suffered lots because of me. Where is Jim?"

Person on the throne: "Jim's time has not yet come. He will come later. You are here because you trusted in me. I AM JESUS. Al and Betty; well done my good and faithful servants." (Jesus stands and gives each in the group a hug and a greeting of welcome)

Guide: "Follow me." (the group follows through a door to a room of chairs and are seated. They are challenged with the gospel to repent if they had not already done so. Several meet with counselors to do just that.

The Drama came to an end. Angels in Heaven were no doubt joyful.

Ben helped in the dismantling of the scenes after the third evening's showing. On that evening Becky stayed home with Daniel. Mark and Melinda were counselors after they had seen the drama themselves, and doing so until all three night's performances were completed.

After Mark finished counseling on the last night, he sought out Ben. "Guess how many came through?"

"Oh, about four hundred?"

"Five hundred fifty three!"

"How busy were you?"

Mark stretched out his arms, putting a hand on each of Ben's shoulders, and smiling announced, "Fifty-five new Christians!"

"You ought be tired."

"I am too excited yet, but I'd bet that Melinda and I will sleep like babies tonight."

"Want me to do your sermon tomorrow?"

"Heavens, no! I hope some of the new ones will come. I am too excited to rest yet!"

"Sorry about not including the kids in the acting parts in this."

"Next year can cover that," Mark said. I have had a sneak peek into a possibility for them. As for you and Becky, well done, my good and faithful friends!"

Chapter thirteen
The Kids' Experiment

Sometimes Nick and Sandy would get together to study. It wasn't so much that they always studied the same subjects. They just liked to be together while doing their homework. Nick's little sister was much younger, and besides that she was, after all, a sister. Sandy was an only child. Now that Sandy was attending Nick's church and a believer, that too was a common bond. One of their parents was always present in the house. Which one it was depended on whether they were at Sandy's home or Nick's.

Nick had invited Sandy, Jody's daughter, to watch the drama with him that their community performed. The two of them were so enthralled with the plot that they wanted to experiment with the possibility of building a drama of their own. They talked about this possibility before, and even more so after they had seen the drama. The adult drama was good, they agreed, but could they make one for the youth?

"Have you had any ideas on where to start?" Sandy asked Nick one afternoon when they did not need to be studying.

"Just a trial outline," Nick told her. "We probably need some of the good kids to think they are good enough, don't you know."

"You are right about that."

"One of them could have been like I was," Sandy said. "I planned to be as good as I could be at everything I did. My grades were good and I was trying to be athletic."

"I too studied hard," said Nick. "And I found I could sing on key most of the time. I did not apply myself to sports with reckless abandon, because, well, I somehow did not like competing where games ended with winners feeling great, and losers down in the dumps."

"I watched you in the games you played. You were the most sincere when you said "Good game!" to your opponents. I didn't ever know what else you said to them, but I noticed some frowns turn to smiles. What were you telling them?"

"It varied. What I said was my game plan. Whether they won or lost, I wanted them to be glad they came, and give it their all."

"It made me feel good too, just watching you."

"Thanks, I had no idea you were watching. Say, could we use some of those thoughts in our story, if we get around to writing one? Before we go any farther, I want to tell you Miss Sandy, I really enjoy sitting and talking with you."

"Nick! Cut it out! You will have me in tears and we will never get this done. But since you brought up the subject, you are the only grown-up acting kid in school, and church too."

"Is it even possible to make progress on this, when my desire is to give you a kiss?"

"Well, mister, get it over with, so we can get back to work." Then she giggles. And he did (kiss), a small one.

"That is all for now," he said.

"Felt good. Hope you have more later."

"Can't give them all away on one night. By the way, all I have in storage have your name on them."

"I will be patient, then. Even getting to sleep tonight after the first one may be difficult."

"That bad, huh?"

Sandy slaps Nick's shoulder, then gave him a hug. Her eyes told him the rest.

"Drama. We need to think drama."

"We had better not make it this good," Sandy proposed. "It has to have bad parts to challenge unbelievers."

"How about I write the good parts and you write the bad parts?" Nick offered.

"You can't get off that easy, mister."

"OK, do we need any car crashes?"

"Let's not, unless we just have the sound effects of one."

"That could work. What were they doing out driving around?"

"Opportunity and independence. Their home lives were a shambles. Her father was a drunk and his father was a brutal disciplinarian."

"She was suppose to be out with the girls, and he had his folks' car to come home from basketball practice."

"He drove by the girls' party, after phoning the girl. She grabbed her coat and slipped out. He picked her up. They drove out onto country roads where they hit a large deer, which did much damage to the car."

"Did he take the girl back to her party? And did he report the accident. Did he get in heaps of trouble, and what did the parents do? Nick, do we want to go this direction?"

"Sandy, this could happen. You know it could. This is what I am asking myself: Are we capable to make it come out all right?"

"I just had a thought: The boy called 911, trying to be legal and let it slip that the girl was with him. The police call the parents. The kids were taken to the police station." Sandy continued. "Two fathers got in cars or pickups and headed furiously to town. One was drunk and the other was beside himself with anger. They collide at the crest of a hill and one or both of them died."

"The kids got a rude awakening, and gave their lives to the Lord, repenting of their bad judgment. They try to forget their situation, and yet keep on making youthful mistakes. They still have haunting feelings of how things could have been even much worse."

"This could jolt kids to be wise in their actions, or we could go another direction."

"Let's sleep on it," Nick said. "It is getting dark outside, so this better be put on hold."

"Be careful driving home. And speaking of hold, could I have another kiss at my door?"

"If I can still drive straight after we do." He promised to call her as soon as he got home, and he kept that promise.

"Good! Thanks for calling. Come back again some time."

"You know I will, and hey! I had another drama idea come to me on my way home; not that this one was bad."

"What was it about?"

"A mother with four or more children and a father which they seldom saw, and some sort of a plot by the kids to get them back together; and it comes together just before Christmas."

"Sounds good. What is the kids' plan?"

"Could you think of one?"

"If I could, I would have already, for my own situation."

"Oops! Sorry. I forgot about that."

"That's OK, and besides that, if we can come up with a good one along that line, maybe it could work for me."

"If it did, it would be worth all the effort. I cannot imagine not having two parents full time."

"I am use to it, but that does not make it good. Would this have any death or judgment?"

"Let's just have near death in it; just enough to rattle some cages."

"Sounds challenging, yet alluring. Of course we could never come up with anything good without getting together to plan it."

"For sure! Well, X's and O's for now. Think about it for a week."

"This could make a great school play, if we can pull it off."

"We will need to use the school stage, with the curtains separating the scenes. We can still have a tour guide, or several if we choose."

"True. This doesn't discourage me. How about you?"

"Not at all. And we could even use a lot of students. As the scenes change, so can the students doing the acting."

"It would tell the whole story without anyone having to learn boocoos of lines."

"Hey! We were suppose to be together to do this!"

"Yeah! This could take a long time, especially if we have a lot of homework to do first."

"We had better get some sleep. Thanks again for this evening. X's and O's back to you."

Chapter fourteen
The Kids' Drama

At first, Sandy and Nick banter about ideas that each of them came up with on their own. Finally they start on a subject that mainly featured children, and using children as all of the characters. Three times together, one evening each week, and the script was written, ready to present to the school. Nick got permission to meet with Mr. Kirkland after school and he told Sandy. "I will drive you home after we talk with him."

When the two entered Mr. Kirkland's classroom, he welcomed them.

"Come in! Have a seat. What is going on?"

Nick spoke first. "Mr. Kirkland, Sandy and I were talking about the drama that was put on for three evenings in our town recently."

"Yes. I heard about it, but I let things get in my way all three nights."

"We wanted something for our age to do along those lines, and together we put one on paper."

"Good! When will it be presented?"

Nick took the lead. "That we don't know, and that is one reason we asked to see you."

Sandy spoke. "We thought that what we came up with would make an excellent school play."

"And you want my permission?"

"Yes," Nick and Sandy said at the same time.

"Is that it in your hand?"

Nick handed the copy to the teacher.

"And you would like to know how soon?"

"It contains a Christmas timing as it is now written," Sandy told him. "That could easily be changed if necessary."

"May I have this over the weekend and get it back to you, say on Monday?"

The two agreed, thanked Mr. Kirkland, then left.

"You know, a year ago I am sure we would have been refused."

"Why?"

"You heard him talk about bullying in one of our pep rallies?"

"Was that you he was talking about?"

"Yes but it was my dad that helped him mostly, and God."

"I should have guessed."

"We have another hurdle to cross after Mr. Kirkland."

"Getting our only copy of the script back?"

"That too."

"The principal?" Sandy guessed correctly.

"At least; maybe all the way to the top."

"Help!" Sandy yelped.

"It is not impossible. We wrote about the possibilities in the script, remember? Let's turn it over to God and let Him bring the walls down."

"We would be hypocrites if we didn't, after the play we wrote." Sandy noted. "Hey! Let's make a pact between us, to give it to God, and not worry another moment about it."

Monday came and Mr. Kirkland gave a message to Nick for him and Sandy to meet him after school, and that he approved, but it had to clear school policy and please those above him.

"So I do not know when I can give you an answer. I have tentatively picked students to try out for the parts."

"You do think it will happen?" Sandy asked.

"I think God gave you two this drama. He guided the rock that brought down Goliath." The phone rang and Mr. Kirkland answered it. Nick and Sandy rose to leave. Mr. Kirkland motioned for them to stay.

"Kirk here....I am talking to a couple of my students....yes, those two....Would our school policy allow it?...state policy? ...It does? Great! No, I can't see it promotes a religion, just faith and hope. Don't all religions have that?... That's what I meant, all we have around here. Could we schedule it before the Christmas break?...

That just might work really well. I will get started on it. You decide if we need the Patriot Guard or somebody to ward off the ACLU....No, I don't either. Thank you, and the two will be saying thank you too." The phone conversation ended, and Mr. Kirkland promised to run copies of the script, advertise for characters and make practice times available.

Nick added, "And the walls came down."

"Yes, they did." Mr. Kirkland agreed.

Semester tests were scheduled for January, so that left some time for practice. Twenty nine students volunteered to learn lines. Nick and Sandy would be Tom and Kim in the last scene. It was decided that due to its brevity, it would be used as a climax to the annual Christmas program. Would that be all right with them? Yes, it was. Mr. Kirkland did not scold the two when they gave each other a small congratulatory hug right there in the classroom. Instead, he gave each of them a hand shake. The crowd of watchers, they surmised, would be likely large, because the Christmas programs always drew a good turnout each year.

Chapter fifteen
The performance

Even though a good-sized crowd assembled to see the Christmas program and the play that Sandy and Nick had put together, the two respectfully asked to not be displayed to the audience as the authors. Mr. Kirkland, although wanting to give credit where credit is due, granted their request. He never promised to not give extra credit to their grades as they come out at semester.

The drama began when a student stood between the stage curtain and the front edge of the stage, introducing it in this way: "Tom, Tim, Ted, Kim, Kelly, and Samantha had a dilemma. They were brothers and sisters, living with their mother, mostly remembering their father by the ever-present picture of him as it rested on the fireplace mantle. Tim and Kim were twins as well as Ted and Kelly. Tom was the oldest sibling, and Samantha the youngest. "Sam" had not remembered her father at all. Tom, although the oldest, didn't have any father-son activities that he recalled with fondness. Let's catch some of the children talking:

Scene one curtain opens

Sam "Kelly, what is Daddy like?"
Kelly "Oh, he's about five feet ten or maybe six feet and has strong hands."
Tim "I remember him as busy all the time."
Ted "Mom says that his work moved him to another state."
Tom "Do you believe that?"
Kelly "I use to, but now I am not so sure. He sends money to Mom each month."
Kim "Do you think Mom is covering for him?"
Tim "I saw Mom holding his picture and tears running down her face."
Sam "She must still love him."
Tim "How can you love someone you never see anymore?"
Tom "I use to pray every night that he would come home."
Kelly "Really? Me too! It has been several years, I suppose, since I prayed that way."
Tim "How long has it been?"
Sam "I am eleven and I don't remember him at all."
Tim "Then it must have been nine years or more."
Kim "Would we even know him?"
Ted "Would he even know us? At best he might just stop in and then leave again."
Tom "I think we should decide on a plan and then make a pact among ourselves."

Sam "What is a pact?"
Tom "It is a plan that we all agree on."
Tim "What might that be?"
Tom "Let's think on it for a few days and all get together again like we are now."

Curtain closes on scene one

Guide, in front of curtain: "Did they all agree on that? Some were uncertain that it was worth pursuing. For the sake of their sad mother, they pressed on to give it their best shot. Now we open to scene two, a week later."

Curtain opens (different actors representing the six children)

Tim "Has any of us come up with anything, or are we back to square one?"
Tom "I think we ought to include someone else in our planning."
Kelly "Who, Mom?"
Tom "No, God."
Ted "God? Anyone heard from Him lately?"
Kim "Has anyone talked to Him lately?"
Kelly "I haven't, and that is my fault. I think Tom is right. Any suggestions?"
Sam "I have one!"
All "You?"
Sam "I may be the youngest, but do you want to hear it?"
Ted "Why not. None of us seem to know what to do."

Kim "Whatcha got, Sam?"
Tom "I'm all ears."
Sam "Let's do the Jericho thing."
Tim "Jerry who?"
Sam "Jericho! Haven't you heard of Jericho?"
Tom "Josh did."
Ted "Josh?"
Tom "Joshua. Go ahead Sam. Lay it out for us."
Sam "Are you all listening?"
All "Yes!"
Sam "Tom, what was that word you used?"
Tom "Pact. We need to make a pact."

Sam "That's it! Let's pact to each pray, each day for six days, not talking to each other about it any of those six days."

Kim "And then all get together on the seventh day and shout?"

Ted "Lord, are you serious......I mean, Sam, are you serious?"

Sam "I don't know about the shout, but on the seventh day we make a pact prayer and all pray it together..........really together.......voice, heart and everything."

Tim "It could work!"

Tom "No, Tim, it will work. We need to all believe right now, it will work."

Kim "Sam, may I work with you on the pact prayer? I heard something in Sunday School that makes sense to me."

Sam "OK."

All "Let's do it!"

Curtain closes on scene two

Guide: "Jericho: The Israelites crossed the Red Sea on dry land, a roadway through the waters. For forty years they wandered in the land around Mt. Sinai, then led by Joshua, crossed the Jordan River. This found them in the Jericho front yard. Before they marched around Jericho, Joshua was told by the Angel of the Lord, that the battle against Jericho had been won. Joshua believed God and in the appointed time Jericho was defeated. After six days of prayer, the six siblings got together again."

Curtain opens to scene three

Tom "Did you all pray each day?"
All "We did."
Tom "This is the seventh day. Kim and Sam have something for us."
Kim "Sam and I looked at Joshua and Jericho. Joshua was not the winner at the Battle of Jericho. God and His Army was. Of course the people of Jericho saw only the Israelites. Their fear was so great that they were easily defeated. Sam?"
Sam "God is in charge of our Jericho. The walls between our father and us are about to fall. We have already won. Dad is on his way. Here is our shout: (Sam passes out slips of paper to each of the six siblings)
Kim "Read what is on the papers. Nod when ready to read it out loud, together. (they read and each

nod…..Unknown to them, their mother was, and had been, listening to it all)

Kim "Together now:"

All "God, we believe you are now bringing this family back together. Thank you for putting Daddy on the road that leads back to us. Thank you for doing what we cannot do. Give us the faith to believe until we see what you have done. Amen!" (the children had a group hug)

The telephone starts ringing. Mother comes into the room and answers the phone.

Mother "Yes, this Martha….Yes, he is my husband….OH, NO!…. OK, we will be there soon." she hangs up the phone. "Kids, Your father was in a bad car wreck somewhere close to our town. He is in the hospital. It may be our last time to see him alive. Quickly, get your shoes and coats!"

Curtain closes on scene three

Guide: "This last scene is at the hospital." The curtain will open to scene four. "Jim is bandaged head to toe, lying motionless in bed. A nurse sits beside him, writing in his chart. The family arrives at the hospital and is shown to Jim's room. Is this indeed the last chance the children get to see their father? Is this any way for God to answer their prayer of faith? I believe they are ready for us to take a look at what they experienced."

(A nurse opens room door and lets family in. The family gathers at the bedside, Mother, then kids in descending age order)

Nurse "Jim!"

Jim(waking) "Yes?"

Nurse "Someone here to see you."

Jim (seeing Martha) "Martha!" (he tries to turn to her)

Nurse "Be careful, Jim."

Jim (to nurse) "This is my wife. And could these be my children?"

Martha "That's them, Jim."

Jim "One, two, three, four, five, and six. Wait……see if I can name them: Tom, Tim, Kim, Ted, Kelly, and could this princess be Samantha?"

Martha "We are all here for you, Jim."

Jim "Yes, you are. And do you know why I'm here?"

Martha "The accident?"

Jim "No, I mean, why I came to town."

Martha "To see us, I hope."

Jim "I know I have some broken bones from the accident, but before I came, I was up on my mountain, and in the middle of the night, my mountain of pride crumbled and became nothing but dust. I want a chance to slowly win back your confidence, no matter how long it takes, even if it takes a long time. Make me prove it. Don't take my word now."

Martha "We will take a vote: Kids, does Jim get another chance?"

Kids "Yes!"

Jim "You want me? Nine years gone, and you want me?"

Kim   "Promise you won't leave us again."
Jim   "Thank you God! No! I will not leave you ever again!"
All   "Thank you Jesus!"

Curtain at close of play (all the cast gather on stage and curtain opens one last brief time)

Cast   "Merry Christmas!"
Audience   "Merry Christmas!"
Cast   "God bless us, everyone!"
Kirk felt tears forming. He wasn't alone.

Chapter sixteen
Movie?

Becky met Ben at the door as he came in from his day's work. Not that it was uncommon for her to do that. This time there was another purpose.

"You have a phone call coming at eight tonight."

"Did they say who?"

"A Mr. Winters. He was quick to explain that he was not selling anything."

"Good."

"Supper is ready if you want it now."

"OK, Daniel, let's wash our paws."

"I don't have paws, Daddy." Ben chuckled.

****

The phone call came right at eight. Ben took it himself. "This is Ben."

"Ben, Wesley Winters. I assume your wife told you to expect a call."

"She did."

"The reason I called is this: I happened upon your story. No, I was given your story to read by a friend. The reason he wanted me, specifically, to read it is, as he said, 'This would make a great movie!' I read it and I agree."

"Thank you."

"I would have been reluctant, since I get that often from those seeking instant wealth. You see, that is what I do."

"What?"

"Take really good stories, and make them into movies. Anyway, I trusted my friend, and he was absolutely right."

"You want a part of my life made into an actual movie?"

"No doubt about it. Initially what I need is your permission."

"It would have to be more than that. I am fully employed. Clearance would have to be obtained from my employer before I could give you the go ahead."

"We wouldn't have it any other way. Would you seek permission for me, providing you yourself are willing? We would want you to approve the script; that privilege we won't revoke."

"Sounds exciting, however, I don't want to be hounded by the media to the extent that I lose my private life."

"In that case, we could change all the names, and bend the story enough to be a work of fiction, somewhat."

"You can do that?"

"Mr. Reed, again I say, that is what we do. But more than just for a story, we have been enamored with your character, your attitude, and your concern for your fellow man."

"Will it matter if my faith in my God is obvious in the movie?"

"Ben, if we intentionally edit out your faith, or if we detect that you are just a big show-off with a big ego, and that God has no part, then at that point I will regret that we undertook this project."

"Can I assume then, that you are a believer also?"

"Heart soul and cowboy boots."

"Well then, I will see what I can do. I cannot at this point make any promise except that I will try."

"Good! As far as how lucrative this might be for you or other helpers, it depends on the cost and the popularity at the box office. Do you need to write down my number?"

"Ready," Ben wrote it and the two men ended their conversation.

"Wow!" Becky exclaimed. "Is this for real?" Both sides of the conversation was loud enough that she heard it all.

"Maybe. Are you in favor of it? Of course, this involves you as much as it does me."

"I will have to admit, it has me going. I just hope we do not regret it."

"There is so much we don't know, since we have not traveled this road before. What my boss says tomorrow is the first of what we need to know. The rest of it may only be the red tape."

Chapter seventeen
Ranger School

Ben did call the state forestry office the next day, telling them about Wesley's proposal to make a movie. His supervisor listened politely, then said. "I have something to talk to you about also, so could I meet with you at your office at about nine Monday?"

Ben's boss did come as promised. Ben showed him the daily log he had been keeping. The man tried to act interested, but he really had other fish to fry.

"Is the truck still running good?"

"Yes. No oil usage either."

"And the tractor and mower?"

"Same. The last oil changes should get them through the winter. I just got this in the mail this morning. It is from the fellow I told you about." The supervisor took the letter and quickly read it.

"Strange how things can sometimes work together." he said after reading the letter.

"How is that?"

"We have the opportunity to get a young man that has been training for forestry service. He needs to spend a year under supervision on a working range. Yours was the first to come to mind. He has a semester remaining after that ,before he is finished completely, ready for placement in an area of his own. Since you have an opportunity to do this other thing, would it be spreading you too thin to do both at the same time?"

"How responsible is the kid?"

"He comes with high recommendation. He keeps up his assignments at or ahead of schedule, the school says."

"Drinker, smoker, or into pornography?"

"They say no."

"City boy?"

"Definitely not. He comes from a family that has enough boys to run the farm after they graduate high school and Dad retires. This one is the least enthused about that kind of farming.

Do you want to do both the movie and the teaching?"

"It may take all summer, off and on, to film the movie, I would expect. It also depends on whether I am needed to play myself in the movie. If the boy works out, would I get a chance to use him in the winter, while we film the winter scenes?"

"As I said, this a full-year assignment. Having him do the summer stuff, not knowing if he can handle the winter complexities, makes him useless to us."

"Yes, I am willing , if you are," Ben stated.

"All systems are 'Go' from this end."

"When does he arrive out here?"

"He is supposedly packed and ready; chomping at the bit. We may lose him to another assignment if we delay. Sorry about not giving you longer notice. Is tomorrow all right?"

"Send him. His name?"

"Grant Hollister."

"From the Hollister Dairy?"

"That's right. Maybe he can take over the job of milking the deer."

"He would have to be fast enough to catch them first."

The conversation ended with well wishes. Ben informed Becky; she had not been able to hear because his boss had met Ben at the range office. He also informed Wesley. And yes, Ben was definitely wanted to play himself in the movie.

"Get to growing your beard while we get set up to shoot. I will be out in a week or so to scout the area."

****

Ben barely got to the range office the next day before Grant came driving in in his old-model Toyota pickup. They met in the parking area.

"You must be Grant. I am Ben."

"Yes, Grant Eugene Hollister. Just call me Grant, please."

"Well, come on in. You had breakfast?"

"Colonial at the motel."

"You didn't start from home this morning?"

"No, I got to town at about seven-thirty last night."

"Wish I had known. You could have come on out then."

"I did not want to start out by being rude."

Ben showed Grant the office and sleeping quarters, and allowed him time enough to move in. He called Becky to see if she could set an extra plate for lunch at noon. She would, of course.

"If you are ready, let's take a short tour of the range." With Grant, Ben drove his usual inspecting route that he tried to run each week, to survey the over two-hundred-thousand acre range.

"Five and a half days a week will be full time. Ask permission for any time you will need to be away, except for runs into town for range purposes. You may use Old Red for everything except personal trips, and not use range fuel in your own vehicle. Becky will have lunch ready for us today. We will go to town and stock up on groceries and other things you will need after we eat. Do you cook?"

"I am not a chef, but good enough to keep myself healthy. I cooked in college, except for the first semester. Going out all the time got too costly."

"The range will provide you the staples, and a list of those staples. We will stock up for a week at a time. A weekly trip in, to replace what you have used, should be all that is necessary. Any extravagance is out of your pocket."

"May I have visitors?"

"Not too often, too long at a time, and not overnight."

"I have a friend who might come out."

"Her name?"

"Mandy. She was my high school sweetheart. College separated us somewhat, and this will too, for the most part."

"Be wise about it. Don't let it distract you from our routine."

"It won't, I promise."

Becky had a simple lunch ready. She was impressed with Grant's manners and his appearance. It did not take long for Daniel to warm up to him. Grocery shopping was in order for the first hour or so after lunch.

Chapter eighteen
Seeking Wisdom

Pastor Mark took the phone from his wife. His eyes asked her who he was to be talking to.

"Ben."

"Ben, Mark."

"Hello, brother. I need to bounce a question off somebody, and you were chosen from a crowd of one."

"Hey! You know as many answers as I have."

"OK, maybe I should have said, I need rebuke or confirmation."

"All right, shoot. What are you wanting my opinion about?"

"About the movie."

"Whether it is of God, and for God?"

"Exactly; am I suppose to do it?"

"Let us count what we know. You did not ask for it. The means to make it happen has been provided. Scenes are in place. One thing we must remind ourselves: we must not drop our responsibilities to our families and employers, making the movie the thing of priority."

Ben was quick to respond, "Yes, I have reminded myself of that. Hey, thanks. Speaking of responsibilities, I had better go spend a day with my junior ranger. He may need some confirmation too. I appreciate your insight. Thanks."

"Any time. I doubt if you needed it."

"I wanted to stay grounded. See you Sunday."

"Bye."

Chapter nineteen
Oops!

Ben got into Big Red and drove to the office. As the small building came into sight, so also did another scene. Grant's girlfriend was leaving the area in her car.

"No!" Ben said aloud. He drove onto the parking lot and got out. Grant met him at the door.

"You saw?" Grant asked.

"Care to explain what I did not see?"

"I had better. We were watching a movie until late and went to sleep sitting on the couch. When we awoke, it was past midnight. I know my promise to you, and I had to weigh that against common sense. To send her away at that time of the morning, whether to your house or to the highway, seemed to be unthinkable. So I got her some blankets, then went to my bedroom, until about an hour ago."

"You do know that breeds temptation?"

"We didn't."

"But."

"Yes, I know, and it was unwise. And," Grant continued, "We were tempted."

Ben thought for a moment. "Follow through now. Call and make sure she made it home all right. Explain why that will never be repeated. Our unawareness left us not encouraging you to do right."

"My fault. She drove in unexpectedly shortly before eleven, but not much before; said she was lonely. I didn't want to bother you at that time of night, nor did I want to be cruel to her. I will gather my things and be gone."

"No, the first thing you need to do is eat breakfast. I'll be back to get you in a few minutes."

"You mean, I can stay?"

"Today is a brand new day. God's mercies are new every morning, so mine should be too, this time."

"Yes sir! Thanks!" Grant dashed into the office. Ben drove home to get some breakfast himself.

At his house again, Ben first sat down at his desk and picked up his daily devotional. This he usually did each morning before breakfast. For this morning this is what he read: I Corinthians 4:7 "For who maketh thee to differ from another, and what hast thou that thou didst not receive? Now if thou didst receive it, why dost thou glory as if thou hadst not received it? Let none of you be puffed up for one against another. Now some are puffed up. Set your affections on things above, not on things on the earth."

"Colossians 3:12 "Put on therefore, as the elect of God, holy and beloved, bowels of mercies, kindness, humbleness of mind, meekness, longsuffering. Knowledge puffeth up but charity edifieth."

Extended reading included all of First Corinthians chapter thirteen.

Ben was convicted so much that he left the house, walking to the edge of the yard. Dropping to his knees, he leaned forward onto his elbows pleading to God, "Lord, forgive me! I have become way too important in my own eyes. I was about to turn my back on what I should be doing. Becky needs more of me. Daniel needs more of me. And now Grant needs more of me. This movie thing is wrong, WRONG! God, help me to be wise, starting now." Ben couldn't find the words to continue.

Becky heard the house door close and she got out of bed. She looked out, seeing that the new pickup was still in the driveway. She opened the front door and saw Ben on his knees. Slipping on some shoes, Becky rushed to Ben's side, dropping to her knees also. Ben turned to Becky, giving her a tight hug. He still couldn't find words to speak.

Becky, in like manner held her man tightly. She had no idea what had taken place so that Ben would be so grieved. Not saying anything, she let him take his time before he was able to speak.

"I'm sorry, Becky," was the first thing Ben managed to utter.

"For what?"

"The movie. It's wrong."

"No, it isn't!"

"It's wrong for me." Ben gave himself a few seconds, then continued. "I was getting too puffed up for your good and even for my own good."

"Let's go to the house. It is too chilly to talk out here." Ben had not noticed. Hand in hand, they returned to the house. They sat on the divan.

"I don't understand," Becky managed to say, starting from where they left off outside.

"Let me show you." Ben got his devotional and handed it to his wife. She read the words that Ben saw earlier.

"Why is this meaning that you are doing wrong?"

"It (the movie shooting) was going to take me away from all I care about, all I should be caring about. It could have put Bob back on a guilt trip. (Bob was the tutor that had persuaded Ben to go hang gliding in which Ben's life was nearly snuffed out) As far as that part of our lives, it is over. To reopen it again would only be self-aggrandizing."

"I guess I can see what you are saying."

"And there would be the obvious temptation to continue the story of our lives in which more people would be involved and hurt. They would not want their past exhumed and reexamined." "Oh, I can see now. Even using Claude and Relda's past to do the drama was a bit of the same thing."

"It was wasn't it? I had better call Wesley." (the movie maker who was in charge of the proposed movie)

Becky proclaimed, "Benjamin Reed, you did it again."

"Did what?"

"Gave me another reason to love you."

Narrow Is The Way   *Lowell Gridley*

****

Wesley Winters listened to Ben as he explained his selfish ambition and how it might hurt others that were involved. Wesley listened politely.

"I just feel as if we can still do this, even if we need to bend the story to minimize the hurtful effects."

"How could we do that?"

"To begin with, picture this: A fellow went hang gliding on his own; by himself. The sudden burst of wind took him away just like it did. When he failed to return home, then the search began. Bob would not have been responsible, and the movie could continue as planned."

"Yes, but…..I would still be neglecting my family and my job if I was a part of it."

"Then don't be a part of it, except to fill me in on the things you did through the ordeal so that I can still build a realistic story. You would be tremendously missed, very much so, but it would not be a movie stopper."

"I get it. To be perfectly factual, it would be in the theaters two months straight to play it all as it really happened."

"Yes, now you do have a handle on it. There are all sorts of ways to make it work, and even change enough to make it hardly recognizable, if necessary. I do not see any reason to do much of that."

"Let me talk it over with Becky and call you back tomorrow,"

Ben thought about the making of the movie all day while he and Grant were working. Neither he nor Becky would be harmed by its production, and Becky would be in it too, if she wanted. Taking Bob out of the picture? He had better ask Bob about that, then let him work it out with Wesley.

Chapter twenty
Snow Rescue

Some of the firewood cutters had come out the designated Saturdays. Grant and Ben had ready for them a few more dead trees in two spots. The clean-up afterward had been minimal. Grateful people show their gratitude by not leaving a huge mess for others to clean up.

A Norther came in early during the night, leaving some snow drifts and a bitter chill. It was a shock to some who were enjoying an unusually warm fall. Very early, the morning of the blizzard, Ben was aroused from sleep by the ringing house phone.

"Ben, this is Blake (Sheriff Blake). We may need your help."

"Name it!"

"Got a call late last night. Some folks are missing who were traveling after thanksgiving. The roads are terrible and the wind chill is in the teens."

"Where have you looked, and where are they likely to be?"

"We have looked half the night along all the places they were most likely to be. They are not on the main roads or in the ditches along them."

"In other words, snow-blinded and lost. How many?"

"Father, mother and two small children; kids ages four and six."

"I'll see what I can find. Is 911 working?"

"Yes. Give me your cell again."

Ben told the sheriff his mobile number. He filled Becky in, dressed fast and stuffed a few biscuits into his pockets as he headed for the door.

"Sleeping bags?"

"They're at the office. I'll get 'em." Grant had been excused to go home for a visit.

Ben got into his newer pickup, not taking time to install the plow on Rover. "Time's a wastin'," he told himself. "Lord, where do I go first," Ben prayed after he had gotten the three sleeping bags. He drove toward the highway. Seeing nothing out of the ordinary, He took off on a tributary road from the driveway out into the forest. It also revealed nothing, so he kept branching off and looking as best he could in the swirling snow. Finally he saw a faint glow and recognized it was his lights reflecting from a taillight of a marooned vehicle.

Ben trudged through two-foot drifts to the car. It was not running. Ben tapped on a door glass. A figure rolled down the glass. "Are you OK?"

"Got one blanket," the mother said. "The kids are cold…….very cold."

Ben pushed a wadded-up sleeping bag through the open window. "Have the kids both get in this one bag. You want one?"

"I'll be all right with the blanket and my winter clothes."

"Where is your husband?"

"He went that way to the highway." She pointed.

"The highway is the other way!" Ben told her. "I'll look and try to be back shortly." He knew he could not direct anyone to the spot he found the car. He also surmised it was better not to be dragging three cold bodies to his pickup in case he also get it stuck somewhere.

Finally getting back to his pickup, Ben climbed in and decided on a new direction to travel. The sun was not yet giving a hint of coming up at this point, and the storm showed no signs of letting up. Going as far as he could in one direction, Ben turned the truck around and decided on a new direction. He rolled down the window so he could see better. They were icing up so terribly he couldn't see much through them or the windshield. Spying something in the snow, Ben stopped the truck. He walked down the hill to the left. It was a mostly snow-covered stocking cap lying below some low-hanging sharp branches. No body was nearby.

Ben returned to his truck, pulled out his remaining two sleeping bags, rolled up the window, and made sure he had his phone. He again walked down the hill, trying to guess which way he should look. Finally going behind some bushes at the bottom of the ravine, Ben saw the man. He was not moving. His bare hands were covering his ears.

Ben opened up a sleeping bag and rolled the man onto it. He was still alive. The matching bag he zipped onto the first one, finishing the closure after he joined the man inside. Opening his parka, Ben laid close to the other guy. He called Becky and 911, telling them their approximate location. He put the stocking hat on the man's head, being careful not to bend his ears in case they were frozen. He tried to put a mitten on each of the man's hands but they were so clinched that that was impossible.

After what seemed like a long time, Ben's bed partner moved, and tried to speak. "Cold!" he said.

"Can you feel your toes and fingers?"

"Toes hurt.......fingers hurt."

That could be a good sign, Ben thought. "Got a biscuit here. Can you hold it and eat?"

Finally their hands connected, exchanging the biscuit from one to the other.

"Got to get to my family," the man said, while chewing the biscuit.

"They are OK. Stay here a little longer. Don't rub your skin. You might have frostbite."

Ben opened his phone again, giving a new report. He looked out of the sleeping bag and saw by early morning light just where they were. He gave Sheriff Blake step by step instructions on how to get a rescue unit to his location. About ten minutes later, three men and a stretcher guided by Ben from inside the bag, slid down the hill on the opposite bank. The man was loaded on the stretcher which became a sled pulled by ropes up the steep embankment to the rescue unit.

Ben wadded up the sleeping bags and made it up the other hill to his pickup. It was still running and warm. After driving to the family's car, he walked to it and then carried one child at a time to his truck. Then helping the mother walk through the deep snow, all of them were finally loaded and on their way to the hospital twenty miles away. There they would join their husband and father.

"Looks like the man won't lose any body parts," the doctor told Ben and the wife. He informed Ben that the other three were, for sure, all right. "You did it again Ranger"

"No. God did it again. I'm going home." He called Becky.

Chapter twenty-one
Howard's New Bible

Ben received in the mail a Bible that was the exact same as his own. He and Becky discussed the best way to get it to Howard.

"Could we agree on an evening and take them out for supper?" Becky asked.

"Sounds good to me. I'll call them." Ben looked up the number and called.

"Zergers!"

"Mrs. Zerger. This is Ranger Reed. Is Howard in?"

"Yes, he is." She must not have yet laid down the phone as she shouted. "Howard.......phone!" Ben pulled the phone away from his ear in case she shouted again. She didn't. Ben heard footsteps growing louder until....

"This is Howard."

"Howard, Ben. We got your new Bible today."

"Good! You remembered."

"Could we get together some evening at the Steak House for dinner? ......our treat. Bring your wife. Becky and little Daniel will be with me."

"Saturday would be great. Wait, I'll ask Sarah." Then to his wife, "Sarah, the Reeds are inviting us out for supper. Would Saturday be all right for you?" Ben couldn't make out Sarah's answer. He could still hear Howard's side of the conversation. "I don't know, except Ben has my Bible...His wife and baby are coming....They want both of us....No, Ben's not that kind of guy....please! She said 'all right.' Seven-thirty OK?"

"Suits us. I won't be an embarrassment to anyone."

"You caught that?" Howard stated as sort an already answered question.

"I'll just fill you in on how some of us guys get together once a week, weather permitting and the ladies in another location. We often compare and highlight favorite verses."

"Sounds good!"

"We won't do that Saturday evening."

Howard agreed. "Sounds like a good plan. Say, I heard about your rescue in the snow storm. That must have been quite an adventure."

"A cold one. It turned out good. It could have been twenty degrees colder and not turn out so good."

"OK, see you at the Steak House at 7:30 Saturday. We can pay for our own."

"Wouldn't hear of it."

****

The snowbound family called the Reeds, asking if it would be all right to drop by for a visit sometime in the next two months.

"Do you know where our north driveway is? We have our name on a large sign," Becky informed them. They said they did. "Push the lighted button when you get there, and we'll open the gate. Any time after 7:00 on week evenings. We'll be through eating by then. Save room for popcorn." The call ended.

"I suppose I'm the popper," Ben said.

"Of course! You're the best. I'll butter it." Becky was quiet for awhile, then added, "Some day we might get the Zergers out here with the snow people. What were their names?"

"I guess I never found out. I think the girls are Vicky and Nikki or something like that. I Never heard their last name."

"Where do they live, close to here?"

"I think they were just visiting here from way down south somewhere."

"Maybe we should have offered to feed them."

"We can't feed everybody!"

"I know, but they are special people."

Chapter twenty-two
Nicodemus

On one particular Sunday, Pastor Mark had a unique sermon and a unique way of presenting it. At the close of the first songs and the offering already received, he stood, put on a robe, tying cord around his waist.

"Hello! My name is Nicodemus. How many of you have read in your Bibles about Nicodemus? Pretending that I am he, let me tell you his story. I was a prominent member of the religious ruling class. The religion was the Jewish religion. We were convinced that there was no other true religion; after all, God had called us out since the time of Abraham, Isaac, and Jacob to be His chosen people. So, being the "called out ones," we tended to look down on anyone who were not like us. Then comes this new fellow out of Galilee; Jesus they called him. According to John the baptizer, Jesus' arrival was fulfilled prophecy. He said that Isaiah the prophet, King David, and others had written many years earlier about a coming Messiah. John himself had a good sized group of followers, but when Jesus came along, gaining more followers than he, he was thrilled. He said that was the way it was suppose to happen. John said it this way, 'He must become greater and I must become less.' You see, John was just announcing Jesus' arrival. He was just the voice crying in the wilderness, 'Make straight the way of the Lord.' Isaiah had written it just that way, referring to John's mission. Some of us looked toward Jesus after that, to see what He had to proclaim. The only one that Jesus referred to as mightier than himself was 'The Father.' That told us that He was introducing himself as the Messiah that was foretold; the Christ promised 400, yes, maybe even 700 years earlier. How could this be true? It didn't appear that Jesus was overpowering anybody to put himself on the Kingly throne. Yet all the words He spoke and read from the scriptures of old, sounded so forthright and true. We were convinced, and then we doubted. We again believed, and then we doubted again. I needed to find out for sure. I searched out the place where Jesus stayed at night, and then one night under darkness, I went to see him. I had to know one way or the other what was the truth. Riding the fence between doubt and belief was getting to me. Jesus received me that night, and I greeted him as 'Rabbi' because He was a great teacher, if nothing else. I had seen Him perform miracles, healing many, some of them without even touching them. That told me that He was sent from God and that He was approved by God. Never did He refute God's word, saying that it had errors. At one time after reading the scriptures, Jesus said, 'Today these words of prophecy have become true.' No, I take that back. He said that they had become 'fulfilled.' They were always true, just not fulfilled until the right time. Then He sat down and taught the people. I had questions of my own, some of which I did not want to ask in a crowd. Jesus said, 'Except a man be born again, he cannot see the kingdom of God'. It is like having a greater pair of eyes, I suppose. But what was this 'born again' thing? So I asked Him, how could these things be? I was asking out of the mind of the flesh, lacking understanding. Jesus told of Moses lifting up the serpent in the wilderness on a pole. In the similar way the Son of man, which He called himself, must be lifted up. People who had been bitten by poisonous snakes could look at the brass serpent on the pole and not die of the snake venom. Could it be true that we could look at Him dangling from a pole and not die because of our bite of sin? I now knew more, and believed more, but my understanding was still lacking. Some of the priests believed in Him. They saw how He was the fulfilling of scripture in some way, although not yet having full understanding, which was also my predicament. I trusted His teaching but I still had a lot to learn. Then came the day that Jerusalem was filled with people, coming to celebrate the Passover feast. Jesus came also with His disciples. He went straightway to the Temple where He drove out the moneychangers, overturning their tables, proclaiming, 'God's house is a house of prayer. You have made it a den of thieves.' That did not win Him any points in a popularity contest. I heard that He and his disciples prepared for the feast as did others. One of His followers defected, and sold him out for 30 pieces of silver. Jesus was captured and made to go through an illegal trial. I would not vote against Him. They crucified Him the day before the big feast, and He died. He died! He hung from a pole and He died! I could see it and I could feel it. He died for my sin. He died for your sin.

"Joseph from Arimathea asked for Jesus' body. Together we prepared it for a quick burial in a new tomb which was nearby. We rolled a big stone over the entrance to the tomb. The Passover was hardly a celebration for us. This year the man who was to save us had died, but I guess it had to be. It was according to the scriptures.

"For 3 days and 3 nights, Jesus lay in the tomb undisturbed. Soldiers guarded the grave so that no one could steal the body. Jesus had predicted that event by telling of Jonah in the fish's belly for 3 days and nights. From early on the morning of the 4th day, the tomb was empty. For the next 40 days, Jesus, in His glorified and resurrected body would show himself to individuals and groups of believers and as possible, even unbelievers. I am one of the believers. Then He was taken up into Heaven until the day He returns for His Church. Are you a part of His Church? If you know Jesus as your Savior, that He died for you and is alive, preparing a place for you for eternity, then yes, you are a part of His Church. Come Lord Jesus."

Pastor Mack took off the robe, prayed the closing prayer then sang the closing song with the congregation.

Chapter twenty-three
Bruised and Deflated
(Joy Blocker)

Ben heard a vehicle pull into the parking area of his range office. Looking out the front window he recognized that it was Steven Serpa's truck. Hitched to it was his livestock trailer. When it seemed that Steve was going to linger in the truck before coming to the office door, Ben decided to meet him outside. As he closed the door to the office, he noticed the truck door opening. Steve stepped out and started walking toward him. Ben was prepared to ask what brought him up their way, but the look in Steve's eyes revealed that he was carrying a tremendous load.

"Got a few minutes?" Steve asked.

"Let me call Becky and then I will have lots of time."

"Did you have something you needed to do with her."

"No. I just perceive that we need more than a few minutes and Becky needs to know that."

"Thanks."

Ben did call his wife, only saying that a friend needed to visit with him. "Might be even past noon. I don't know yet."

"I will prepare enough to have him join us, if you want."

"He may agree to that. It is hard to know that too. Don't call the prayer chain, but do pray; it looks heavy, very heavy."

"Sloppy Joes is my plan. Any time is all right."

"I love you. Thanks. I will call; don't know when."

"I'll keep my ears on."

"Thanks, bye."

"Bye."

"Let's drive out onto the range. Be OK to take your truck?" Ben asked. "We need to get away from any interruptions."

"Bless you!"

Ben joined Steve and directed him to a spot that was completely out of sight from all directions.

"Pull in here."

Steve shut his truck off and then gave a deep sigh.

"Let me pray." When Steve nodded, Ben went to the throne room on Steve's behalf, asking for wisdom and courage for the subject at hand. Tears were starting to form in Steve's eyes, and seeing that, Ben's also started forming.

Having said "Amen," Ben asked Steve to unload what he was carrying.

"Just between you and me?"

"And God." Ben added.

"Yes, and God."

Steve sighed again, before trying to arrange his thoughts into words. "You and Becky know some of the struggles Sharon and I have weathered." Ben nodded. He prepared to hear divorce among the next words. It wasn't. "Well, this is no big thing, but it is taking the wind out of my sails. A little while before we were married, I stumbled onto the fact that Sharon was using smokes to help her tangled mind to cope with whatever she was struggling over. I didn't know about the miscarriages yet then, and I did not divulge my discovery to anyone. For me it was embarrassing to my pride but I hung in there, supposing that I was possibly a part of the cause. Well, that seemed to go away, and then we got married. It had not gone away completely, just continued to be covered up. I suppose I should have said something but I was at a complete loss on where to start. Instead I was screaming to God, 'Make it go away!!' I somehow knew that to say, 'Stop......Please!' would be just wasting my efforts. What would you do if Becky was having that problem?"

"I would probably check out of my responsibilities for awhile, and then run off to the mountains to get my head glued back on."

"I did that!"

"And then I would do my best to find a true friend that would help me to approach God for an answer."

"Well, here I am!"

"Yes, and I am both honored to be that friend, and apprehensive that I lack the answers you need. Becky knows Sharon pretty well, and even though she never came out and said it, I am pretty sure she knows some of that about her. Having never tried smoking, because I knew it was unhealthy to do so, physically and spiritually, and not knowing how soon it would be a part of my life style, or an off-and-on addiction, I can only suggest how to unload it to God so you have a chance to get some wind back into your sails, and be able to enjoy life with energy again. I know how much you want to keep all this under cover, for your sake and for Sharon's, but I think Becky could shed a lot of light on what to do."

"I don't want to burden any more than you, and even that may be my weakness, to not just cowboy up and keep truckin'."

"Steve, you are required to make this effort. 'Therefore to him that knoweth to do good, and doeth it not, to him it is sin (James 4:17). Two are better than one because they have a good reward for their labor (Ecclesiasstes 4:9).' We are going to have a good answer for you before we even think of giving up. If I am your only source, besides God, then that might be enough."

"Would Becky be willing to join in the fight; the fight for answers, not the fight against Sharon. Ben, I just want to smile again."

"If I am expected to take sides against Sharon, then even I am the wrong guy. And yes, even if I am to not breathe a word to Becky, I will keep that promise to the letter. The answer to your question as to whether Becky would be willing to help, know this: Sharon is like a sister to Becky, and she loves her sister. She also knows how much you mean to me as a friend. Don't ask me how I know that."

There was silence for a few seconds, then Steve said, "OK, ask her if she wants to help you search for answers. Don't tell her yet who it concerns until she is completely willing, agreed?"

"Agreed, and you are invited to eat our noon meal with us, if you will."

"No! That would be asking too much."

"No. Becky already knows this was possible, and she has already prepared Sloppy Joes to feed at least three. Say you will, please!"

Steve gave it a moment of thought. "You win. Give me forty acres and I'll turn this rig around."

"I have seen you drive. One time I watched you back into a gap that many thought impossible. And what we three are about to do may seem as impossible. It isn't. The answer is on the way. You have never seen Becky and God work as a team. I have, and it is not much short of marvelous."

"Now you have me believing it."

Ben called Becky while Steve drove them back to the range office.

"Yes?"

"Coming!"

"Good! It is ready and I am ready. And I have been given a plan, I think."

"I told him you would!"

"Then I am in the loop?"

"Yep."

"Steve and Sharon?"
"How did you know?"
"Saw you heading into the woods."
"Praise God!"
"Praise God."

Ben told Steve that Becky had seen and recognized his truck and trailer and had been on her knees already for them.

****

Becky met Ben and Steve at the front door, giving both of them a hug. That took Steve by surprise, but only increased his hopes that an answer was on the way. After Ben asked God's blessing on the meal, all four devoured the Joes like they hadn't eaten for days. After being coaxed, Steve ate four of them. Ben ate three, Becky two and Daniel, almost a half of one.

After the meal Becky encouraged Daniel to nap. He dutifully obeyed.

Ben filled Becky in on the problem as Steve had expressed it. She elaborated on what she had received while praying. This would probably involve a conversation that she would have with Sharon herself, explaining how Steve was suffering at her folly.

" I wake up in the middle of the night and my insides are just churning," Steve said, continuing from where he had left off while talking to Ben earlier. "I dream that I am trying desperately to reconnect with her and only getting scoffed at. To her, I seem to be naïve, so out of touch with reality. Jesus said that He came so that we might have life, and life more abundantly. I am getting an abundance of something, but it doesn't feel like abundant life. I even feel like an intruder, coming to your perfect family with my problems. Whenever I believe that the problem is over, and a long time passes, I get a surge of strength only to be cut down like a big oak tree with another discovery. When I get up the nerve to try to discuss a possible way to escape the addictive practice, she senses it and makes an escape, to her computer or something else. It is a small miracle that we had gotten close enough to have Grace. That was before I had made another discovery in the closet, so-to-speak."

Ben had another piece of wisdom to hand to Steve. "This may be one more opportunity for you to trust God's love for you. For we know that all things work together for good to those who love, and trust in God; to those who are the called according to His purpose. So with the faith of Christ we can even thank Him for His provision for us to believe. Unless we know that He is directing us to do or to say a particular thing, we can watch with anticipation what He already is setting about to do. I am ready to see that answer. From now until then, we should thank Him for its coming."

How Becky's visit with Sharon would turn out, they would find out. Sharon might first hear about "Strange fire" being an abomination unto God and the smoke thereof being a separation between God's children. Would she listen and repent, turning her life around, with God's help? Or would she turn her back on her close friend, and much worse, on God?

After talking with his friends, Steve took his truck and trailer and headed home, trying to be patient until Becky felt called to visit Sharon. Becky had, during their visit, shown both Ben and Steve the verse in Acts which showed her that God had his own timing for her to visit: Acts 1:7

About three years had passed since Becky's and Sharon's coloring book conversation. Sharon remembered Becky's advise and had purchased a coloring book and a box of twenty-four crayons. One day it looked like a good time to give coloring a try. Opening to a page that Grace wanted to color, Sharon started coloring the opposing page. She took her time, being careful to stay between the lines and to not color faces, arms, legs and hands some strange color such as blue, green or orange. Grace did not restrict herself under those confines. She randomly colored anything any color, supposedly paying little attention to what her mother was doing.

Over at the Reed home, Becky had been reading the scriptures and came across the one that said, "This is the day which the Lord has made; rejoice and be glad in it. Another of the suggested verses to consider was, "When the time was right, He sent forth His Son born of a virgin." Also was along with those two was a third: "What thou doest, do quickly!"

At noon Becky asked Ben if he thought it was God's prodding her to go see Sharon today. Ben agreed that it appeared to be.

It had now been a couple of weeks since Steve and Ben had visited and Becky had listened.

"Don't rehearse what you will say." Ben said. "God will lead you while you are there. I will watch Daniel." It was Saturday noon and Ben had no work plans for the rest of the day.

Becky didn't waste time, quickly getting ready and leaving for the Lazy S Ranch.

****

"Let's go get the mail," Sharon told Grace.

"I want to do another picture."

"Can you do that while I get the mail?"

"If you don't hurry too fast."

"Color it good"

"Like you do?"

"Yes, do just like I do." Sharon drove to the end of the long driveway, got the mail, looked through it, then turned around, and headed back to the house. After she had stopped, and gotten out of the car, she noticed two things. Another car had just turned into the driveway, and then she heard a blood-curdling scream coming from her house. Just as she was shutting the car door, Grace came running through the front doorway, her hair in a blaze of fire. Sharon used her own coat to smother out the fire.

Not seeing what had happened, Becky brought her car to a stop behind Sharon's and got out.

"Help!" Sharon screamed. Now seeing the problem, Becky quickly ran to Sharon's house, getting a wet towel, a jar of olive oil from the kitchen and then returning outside.

"Put this on her face and hands as we go!" They got into Becky's car and went speedily the five miles to the Hospital. On the open road Becky informed the hospital of their soon arrival, and then she called Steven. He answered.

"Steve! Hospital! Grace!" That was all he needed to know now.

"Be right there!"

Where he had started from they didn't know, but he came to a quick stop while the hospital crew was loading Grace onto the emergency cart. Grace had stopped screaming and was reacting to her frightened mother and watching the nurses as they wheeled her into ER. Steve caught up to Sharon.

"Don't know!" Sharon answered Steve's question before he could ask it. "Hair burned and burns on her face and hands." The parents were told to wait outside ER.

Becky found a private spot, and from there called Ben. "I was sure I was to see Sharon. Guess I was not quick enough."

"And then again, maybe you were."

"How can you think that?"

"I know, that sounded bad. Let's just watch. I probably won't come down. What caused it?"

"Don't know. Sharon left Grace for a few minutes while she drove to the mailbox and back. Grace was coloring in a coloring book, trying to color just like Mommy."

A doctor came to Steve and Sharon. "She was one lucky girl. Just first degree burns on the skin. What you did for first aid kept it from further damage. Her hair was nearly all gone. We clipped off what remained. She told us that she found a fire maker and did just like Mommy."

"Oh, God!" Sharon exclaimed. "She must have watched me sometime."

"Mrs. Serpa, hair spray and fire starters should be kept out of reach of children."

"It was the one in my purse."

"Then you are a......?"

"I'm afraid so, and now because I do, I am almost childless. Steve, I'm sorry; I'm so sorry!"

"What are you going to do now?" Steve asked.

"Take it all away from me!"

"I am not touching them!"

"No, I shouldn't expect you to. I'll do it."

"Until?"

"Never! Never again, ever!"

"Promise?"

"Promise!" then to Becky, "She was doing what she apparently saw Mommy do. Mommy has been very bad!"

Becky asked, "Does Mommy need a whipping?"

"Mommy just got her whipping. It hurts; It hurts bad!"

"I think I am not needed here," Becky said. "I will keep you in my prayers. Let me know."

Sharon turned quickly, and while sobbing, gave Becky a hug. "Thanks! Once again, you were just in time."

"My turn," Steve said. He too gave Becky a big hug, while softly saying into her ear, "God bless you, big sister, for all you've done. We will let you and Ben know the outcome. It looks promising. Sometimes there has to be a train wreck."

"There really does." Becky agreed. She went to her car, called Ben, then drove the twenty-five miles home. Steve was right; when God's children get off track, sometimes there has to be a big train wreck, Hebrews 12: 6-8. Those who are hurting long before the wreck, still must be very careful to not cause the wreck. Much suffering is done in silence. Morning will come. They that wait upon the Lord shall renew their strength; they shall mount up with wings like the eagles. They shall run and not be weary; they shall walk and not faint. Hebrews 12: 11 is good to remember in situations like this; also I Corinthians 10:13.

Chapter twenty-four
A New Friend

The afternoon was pleasantly warm and there was hardly a breath of wind. Ben pulled to a stop at his house in his big red pickup. He turned off the key and went immediately into the house. Becky was reading a book and Daniel was playing on the floor with his red tractor, trailer, and building blocks. The blocks were strewn across the floor except for a small stack right in the center of the room. Ben watched as his son took another run out into the "field" to get a load of "hay bales" with his "heavy equipment." With each load, the stack grew.

A disinterested mother might have scolded her boy for the "mess". Becky was not that kind of mother. She could plainly see that her son was recreating what he had seen his father doing. She caught sight of Ben at the entrance to the room. Seeing his finger at his lips, she knew that he wanted to watch Daniel "at work" before he announced his presence. After three more trailer loads, the "bales" were all gathered and stacked.

"Good job!" Ben said.

"Daddy!" exclaimed Daniel, and he ran to waiting arms.

"You are home early," Becky observed. "Are you going somewhere, or did I forget something?"

"I came to see if you two would go see something with me."

"Now?"

"Yes. I have a new friend and I think it is time for you to meet him too."

"An animal?"

"Yeah. Daniel, I want you to bring your big yellow ball and," to Becky, "Would you bring the camera?" Soon the threesome were in the truck, heading toward the dense forest.

"Here is my plan," Ben informed as they rode. "When we stop, I want us to walk, and at one point, I will have you and Daniel stop while I go a little farther alone."

"Will we be in danger?"

"No. If my friend shows, you won't be harmed ….observed, but not harmed."

"Still or motion?"

"Motion please," Ben answered.

After they had ridden for a few miles, Ben brought the truck to a stop. "We want to appear casual, not sneaky, and not loud." The three got out quietly. They walked to a grassy patch together.

"Are you sure your friend is here?"

"Not completely sure, but I believe he is still in the area. OK, now the two of you stop. It would probably be better if you sit on the ground."

"May we roll the ball to each other?" Daniel asked.

"That might be good, if you are not too far apart." After he had walked another fifty feet, Ben too sat down. He gave something a toss into a large bush, and announced, "Suba, supper's on. I have somebody here to see you." Ben was quiet for a moment then he continued talking. "He's here. Suba, I can hear you sniffing. Your supper is going to get cold if you don't hurry."

Becky and Daniel kept rolling the ball to each other, until Ben spoke to them. "Daniel, roll the ball toward me." Daniel did as his daddy requested. The distance between was too far for the throw. Ben got up, picked up the ball and rolled it back to his son.

"OK, do it again." After another try, the ball was getting all the way to Ben. "Nice throw. OK, pretend I am over by those bushes." Ben pointed to his right. "Roll or bounce it over there." Daniel did. Ben took his time, but went to get the ball, then rolled it back. "Again." Daniel rolled it nearly the same as before. Ben rolled it back. "Now, see if you can get it to go into the bushes."

Daniel stood up and put all his strength into the throw. The ball did go out of sight into the bush. Shortly, Ben heard some more sniffing. The ball was being checked out. Becky was unable to hear it. She aimed her camera at the bush. After seeing that he needed to get the ball, Ben went over, reached into the bush and retrieved it. The ball was damp on one side.

To Becky, "He touched it."

Becky had to know. "What is it, a raccoon?"

"No, Suba is a cougar. He is brownish orange." Ben rolled the ball back to Daniel telling him to roll it to the bush again. Ben proceeded to walk toward Becky and Daniel while the ball was thrown. He then sat with them, noticing that the ball was two feet from the near side of the bush.

"I think it is time. Let's watch and see if he shows." About two minutes later, a long paw and leg projected from the bush. It seemed to be attached to nothing. The ball moved slightly.

"Got it," Becky said softly yet with joy. She had it on film. After another minute, Ben got up, went to retrieve the ball, then rolling it back toward the others.

"Let me roll it this time." Ben knelt, took the ball and rolled it to a spot about four feet from the bush. "Roll it back!" Ben commanded.

"Will it?" Becky wanted to know.

"He's over any fear. Who knows what can happen. The paw came out again, but only reached half way to the ball. It was pulled back into the bush. "I was hoping that would happen." Then the animal crawled almost all the way out of the bush, cupped his paw around the ball, pulling it to himself, then escaping with it into the bush."

The three watched and waited for awhile. When it seemed like the ball game was over, Ben moved to call it off and go home. "I will get you a new ball," he told Daniel. The three were standing and turning toward the truck when Suba let out a growling whimper. The three looked back just in time to see the ball come rolling back out of the bush. "Maybe not!" Ben said, and got the ball.

He had Daniel roll it another time. This time it landed at about the same spot where Ben had picked it up. That was about eight to ten feet from the side of the bush.

"Your turn," Ben called to Suba. A small whine was heard and shortly the whole animal walked out and to the ball. Smelling it once again, and without looking toward the audience, he gave the ball a big whack, sending it bouncing and rolling almost right to Daniel. Suba walked gingerly into the trees to the left side of the bush and kept going until he was out of sight.

"He played catch with me!" Daniel said.

"Yes, he did son; yes he did." Becky had recorded it all.

"He is beautiful!" Becky exclaimed, knowing that her voice was not going to spoil anything. "And big! But he wasn't the white one." Both she and Ben chuckled. Daniel had the only ball in the neighborhood, even in the world, that had been both licked and kicked by a wild mountain lion.

Chapter twenty-five
Small Letters

It had been awhile since Grace had mimicked her mother, and in so doing had caught her hair on fire. Her new hair was as pretty as it use to be, although not nearly as long yet. Sharon had indeed kept her promise, and in addition to being pretty on the outside, she was increasingly pretty on the inside, and she kept a much smaller stash of breath mints. Steve had new joy, and with it, a renewed strength. Every now and then he had one of those nightmares that brought him awake in the middle of the night. After he finally admitted to her what they were about, Sharon got a better picture of what she had put him through for so long. Becky had told her that she needed to draw Steve back to herself more than once, but every so often. A man needs to be loved as often as a woman does. Even if they are strong and brave, which Steve was both, they still need respect and reassurance.

Daniel was four years old, going on seven in several ways. His hunger for learning kept his parents busy supplying the answers. He could print his full name and in addition to that, his mother's and father's. Ben had his part in the teaching of his son. He had remembered that his first grade teacher had used flash cards in teaching his class the basic words found in their readers. He made some for Daniel using his best penmanship, and included words his son asked him about. So far Ben had not had to get the dictionary out to spell any of them.

One day when the weather was too damp for Daniel to play outside, he busied himself with a pencil and some sheets of notebook paper that Becky had given him.

"How do you spell Grace?" Daniel asked his mother. She spelled it for him very slowly. He read it back to her one letter at a time.

"Remember, the first letter is a capital G."

"I have all of them capital," he told her. "Is that OK?"

"I guess it is for now." She presumed he was just writing names. Why had he only asked to spell Grace?

"What is her other names?"

"Her middle name is Elaine," She spelled Elaine for him. "Her last name is Serpa." She likewise spelled Serpa for him. Just before suppertime, Daniel asked for an envelope and a stamp. She held off on the stamp until she was sure he needed a real one.

"Did you write somebody a letter?" and she handed him a small envelope.

"Yes, but I don't know how to mail it so that she gets it."

"If it is to Grace, I know her address. I have sent letters to Sharon. The address is the same.

Daniel gave his mother that "I know that" look, but didn't say it. "Can you help me fold it?"

"May I?" Ben asked. He had been listening. Daniel handed him the letter and envelope.

"Don't read it."

"I won't," Ben told him, but he wanted to.

"I want to lick it," Daniel said. That would insure that nobody would read it before it was mailed.

"Be careful to not cut your tongue on the flap." Ben coached.

"OK."

Becky addressed the envelope and explained the return address. Handing Daniel a postage stamp she told him, "Put it on right side up."

"Like this?" He held the stamp above the upper right hand corner.

"That's right."

Daniel pressed it down and gave it to his mother. "When will she get it?"

"The mailman will pick it up tomorrow and probably it will be in their mailbox the next day." Her little boy was growing up, and not only in stature. As a caring parent, Becky didn't tease. Ben was not inclined to either. It is important to stay connected during the formative years.

"Shall we walk it to the mailbox tonight, after supper?" Ben asked. "The rain seems to be over."

"Can we?"

"You two can," Becky said, excusing herself. "I need to clean off the table and put the leftovers away." She wasn't entirely certain yet, but Becky felt like she might be giving birth to another member to the family in about eight months.

Ben and Daniel donned coats and hats, and with a flashlight each, headed out the door for the long walk down the driveway. Some night animals were out and about. The guys got to see two cottontails and an armadillo, a rarity this far north, but becoming less so with each passing year.

Daniel placed the letter in the mailbox and raised the flag as he had observed his parents do numerous times. He had his light on for most of the walk home. A lot of the time he was shining it in the bushes and trees. While they were gone, Becky had called and talked to Sharon so that she could help her daughter enjoy the surprise of receiving the letter.

Chapter twenty-six
Mine!

Grace rode with her mother to get the mail, discovering that one envelope was for her.

"Oh, my! Who could that be from?"

Grace looked at the only other name on the envelope. "Dan-e-ul……..Daniel! It's from Daniel……..to me!"

"May I see it?"

"Mine!" Grace asserted, clutching the letter to her chest.

"OK!" Sharon conceded. "You want me to read it to you when we get to the house?"

"I know some words," Grace stated. "I will learn more." She had only gotten birthday cards until now. It wasn't her birthday. Her mother had to read those to her. This was different. She was determined to only let Daniel explain this letter to her, if necessary.

Grace dropped her coat on the floor when they got back to the house.

"Is that where your coat belongs, young lady?"

Grace didn't argue. She dutifully hung it up on her nail at the back door entrance. She then made a beeline to her bedroom to open her mail. The letter was a combination of a few words and a few hand-drawn pictures. For instance there were trees (and colored pictures of two trees), a pickup truck (and a colored picture of a truck), the words tree house along with a picture of one of those. There was a second page of words and hand-drawn pictures. No, she didn't need anyone to read to her……..thank you.

Grace asked her mother for some paper and an envelope, after they had eaten supper.

"It appears that our daughter has a boyfriend," Sharon told Steve even before he asked. She got the items that Grace needed.

"Lock the doors," Steve said smiling. "I'm not ready for this."

"Mom, if I put Daniel's name down here (on the envelope), and mine up there, would that get it there?"

"If you write it really well, that should do it." Sharon remembered her first boyfriend. It was in the first grade. They were the only two who wore cowboy boots. Hers were hand-me-downs but boots none-the-less. Her daughter wasn't in kindergarten yet.

Grace got her crayons to make part of her letter. She covered her letter with her upper body when Sharon walked by, on her way to the kitchen for nothing in particular. When she had finished, Grace folded her letter the same way Daniel had folded his, and slipped it into the envelope. After sealing the envelope, she handed it to her daddy.

"Get a stamp from your mother. I will mail it first thing tomorrow morning."

Grace climbed up on the divan, and planted a quick kiss on her daddy's cheek. "Thank you Daddy." Sharon had been too curious, and now she was completely out of the loop. The next day Steve mailed the letter as he had promised. Sharon hoped that she could accidentally find the letter from Daniel. Grace seemed to have hidden it well.

Chapter twenty-seven
Private

"My daughter is very private with her letter from Daniel," Sharon told Becky on one of their phone visits.

"Is it getting to you?"

"Sort of. It shouldn't, I know."

"I think they won't elope until next spring."

"What?!"

"Just kidding." Becky was chuckling. "Actually it is a good way for them to share what they have learned."

"Have you and Ben decided on the home schooling question?"

"Yes we have. We have visited with several families who are planning to home school and we have made a decision to meet once a week as a group for at least one subject so that the children can be use to being with others."

"No preschool?"

"Actually he is past preschool already."

"You are making me jealous."

"You and Grace can easily get to that point. It appears that she is eager. She and you could have a lot of fun this year."

"Does Daniel know most of the alphabet, and a few numbers?"

"Yes, he is on his way to great things." Actually Becky wanted to brag that her son knew all the alphabet forward and backward, in both upper case and lower case. As far as numbers, now that he reached three hundred, he didn't need coached from there on. He was into writing words and soon forming sentences.

When they finished their conversations, Sharon looked out the window in time to see Grace climbing into Steve's truck with a paper of some sort in her hand.

So that's where she is going to hide it. Sharon was pleased that she had looked at just the right time. Grace had even closed the truck door and must have remained inside for quite a while. Too bad it was so far from the house and partly hidden by bushes and trees. What the girl had done in the truck was completely out of Sharon's view. Finally the truck door opened again and Grace crawled out, closing the door behind her. She triumphantly marched to the house.

Sharon opted to not mention to anyone what she saw, and secretly planned a look-see herself when the timing was right. She, for sure, did not want to tell Steve. He obviously could care less about the letter. Steve did, however, see his wife watching out a house window at the same time he heard the truck door shut and see his daughter walking across the spans between the buildings and the house, empty handed. He would let Sharon inform the girl about not playing in automobiles. No reason for her to hear it twice.

Before going to the house himself, Steve went to get his grain feeding bucket, finding it in a spot he had not left it, and upside down. Noting what it was next to, he had to chuckle at the engineering his daughter had created to keep her privacy private. He didn't have to look further to know for sure. He also decided to lock step with his daughter and also to teach a lesson that needed to be learned. He wouldn't even need to be around to watch.

After supper, Steve informed the other two that since no one had picked up the day's mail, he was going to walk the long driveway to get it. "Sugar, do you want to walk out there with me?" The moon was shining brightly; no other lights would be necessary.

"Yes, Daddy! Let's go! There might even be one for me!"

"I guess that is possible. Get your coat."

As father and daughter got out of sight, the predictable took place. Sharon walked toward the barn, opened the truck door that was next to the barn and climbed in. Her eyes saw a pop can on the truck seat and under it a neatly folded piece of paper. Making a mental note of the positions of the can and the paper, so that they could be repositioned, she lifted the pop can, finding that it had been filled with gravel and the bottom was missing. The cab seat was now a mess and there was no time to clean it up tonight.

Completely embarrassed, Sharon ran back to the house. Tears of shame mixed with tears of spite. Surely her daughter had help, and besides that, the paper only had one word on it: "Gotcha!" She figured it best to not even tell Becky. Becky would only laugh at her with the rest of the world. Becky had at one time mentioned that keeping some secrets can eat at you. Yes, Sharon was the owner of one secret, and Grace had the same tendency it appeared.

Daniel enjoyed his letter from Grace. "Some of her spelling is bad," he told his mother.

"She will learn when she gets to school. Her parents may teach her a few things before then."

"What is a satel pokit?"

"A what?"

"Satel pokit. Grace said my letter to her was in a satel pokit. She said it was a seekrit. She drew a picture and colored it brown. See?" Daniel showed his mother the picture. "See? This the satel and beside it is the satel pokit."

"Oh, I know what she is trying to spell, and her secret is safe with me. You might not tell Grace that I know. She may be afraid I will tell someone else. I won't of course."

"Thanks, Mom."

Chapter twenty-eight
Thank You Visit

It bothered Sharon that she had not reinforced her heartfelt gratitude to Becky for her help; first to her wisdom of child rearing, but as of late, her assistance in getting herself and Grace to the hospital. She found time, called Becky, told Steve her intentions, then drove the twenty miles to visit her "big sister." Steve again felt relief that his wife was still on the right road. Looking at Grace, one could never guess what she had gone through with the fire a few months ago.

Sharon drove all the way into Ben and Becky's town-side driveway. It was shorter to have driven to Ben's range office, then cross-country to their house, but not by much. She could have gotten lost out in the forest and rough terrain by going that shorter way.

Becky activated the driveway gate opener after Sharon had pushed the buzzer button at the gate. Soon she and Grace were unloading from their car at the Reeds. Daniel and Grace immediately started playing with

Daniel's toys. This was exciting to Grace because for the most part, her toys were naturally girl toys. Her many things did not include tractors, trailers, dump trucks and excavators. When their small talk seemed to be covered, Sharon finally got to the point of her visit. She was still kicking herself for having been caught up in the destructive habit that nearly got her daughter killed, and could have even burned down their home.

"Another bad thing is that I still have times that I miss that part of my past."

"You did get rid of all that stuff, didn't you?"

"Immediately!"

"That's good!"

"Oh yeah. One of the times that I wished I hadn't was when Steve pulled a prank on me, that I really deserved." She did go ahead and tell Becky about the search for the hidden letter, which she still did not know its whereabouts, and the can of rocks on top of the "Gotcha!" note. "My first inclination after that moment was the desire to light one and show him that he need not mess with me. I had not saved any for those hurtful moments."

Becky had read in one of her Bible studies some verses that she now wondered whether Sharon needed to know. Hoping this to be a nearly perfect time to find out, she told Sharon her discovery, then got her Bible. After turning to 2 Peter 2:20-22, she let Sharon read the words for herself.

"This is gross!"

"Not to the sow and the dog; just to us. It was

natural to them to do what they do. Satan tries his darnedest to get us to return to our mire and to the dog's stuff."

"And I was wanting to get back to my filth just because I felt walked on?"

"Exactly! You wanted a pity party."

"And I had several decisions to make concerning how I had messed up Steve's truck. I could have blown it off, trying to forget it ever happened. I could have cleaned it up the best I could in a poor way, or I could have asked Steve to plug in a shop vacuum so that I could clean his truck well."

"You had another option."

"What's that?"

"You could have flown into a rage and let Steve knew he shouldn't treat you that way."

"After what I put him through, I knew better than to do that."

"You see, if you had saved a little of your ugly past to be available just in case, then that would have been a chance for Satan to use it to get a foot in the door or the camel's nose under the tent to ruin all you had promised."

"Thank God I didn't."

"For sure. One little slip could make all the promises you had made, and the trust that Steve is getting back, or has gotten back, to be all lost, and it all would be worse than at the first."

"But it would have been just one little slip up!"

"You would be willing to have Steve know you went back to lick up your vomit?"

"Becky!"

"Too strong a picture?"

"Yes!"

"Not to Steve. You are fortunate that he is of the forgiving nature. I would never ever wanted to watch you do that, so I can imagine how it would crumble the faith he has regained in you."

"But I am nice to Steve. I do lots of things for him."

"And the dog was probably a great dog. Seeing him re-eat his own food still would leave an ugly memory. You wouldn't want it to immediately lick you on the face even if you know it liked you."

"And I shouldn't have expected Steve to willingly be close to me for awhile, right?"

"Exactly! Even if you had showered, used breath fresheners, and changed clothes."

"And gotten rid of all my stash……..again."

"Now you are getting closer to the whole picture."

"Yes. Yes I am, and it is a big picture."

"It really is."

"And you are going to tell me to give it all to God?"

"All of it. The whole desire. Thank Him for allowing you to have experienced it all so that you could grow."

"Thank Him?"

"Absolutely!"

"Why?"

"So that He knows and you know that He takes everything and works it together for your good."

"And He is not angry?"

"No. He sees the end of it all, even before it started."

"Wow!"

"It's big! Oh, what did you do about the truck and the gravel?"

"I drug my feet too long. Steve had it all cleaned up before I got to it."

"Then?" I gave him a big hug and told him hanks."

"He accepted the hug and gave me a kiss, and smiled; not saying anything."

"Forgiven?"

"Apparently. I cooked him steak and the trimmings for supper."

"Good girl! You did good."

"It felt good. Well, we had better go home and cook another supper. My man will be hungry again."

"It is nice to know that he has an appetite."

"He probably didn't for quite awhile. He just ate to keep going."

"You're getting a better handle on how much he was suffering."

"I think I do now. Thanks to you for showing me the Bible's picture of pigs and dogs."

After a few minutes more of conversation, Sharon and Grace put on their coats and went home. On the way, Sharon mulled over in her mind one of the things Becky had said during their visit. She had talked about who was in control. Sometimes, she said, we get so bent on being in charge that we let ourselves get out of control just so we can be deceived in believing we did it our way. Sometimes we let the other person or people suffer a little so we can maintain supremacy. Had she done that with Steve? She swallowed hard at that thought. It hurt going down. Since the albatross that was around her neck was now both dead and gone, she felt truly free, not having to live the old guarded lifestyle. Old things have passed away. Behold, all things have become new. With the heart man believeth unto righteousness, and with the mouth, (what goes in and what comes out) confession is made unto salvation.

Chapter twenty-nine
Let There Be Lights

Claude caught a glimpse of red and blue flashing lights in his rear-view mirror. They were quite a ways back, but out of habit he quickly took a look at his speed-o-meter. He still had his cruise control set on the speed limit. Instead of passing Claude's truck, the car remained at his rear, even when it got close. Something wasn't right and Claude chose to find out. He dialed 911 on his phone.

"911, what is your emergency?"

"Mabel, this is Claude in my beef taxi. I have a flasher following me, wanting me to pull over. Is it one of ours?"

"I'll check. One, two, three, are you following a cattle truck?"

"Negative on one." They were trained to answer by number sequence.

"Number two; don't see a cattle truck."

"Number three?"

"Just grabbed a doughnut. No cattle truck in line with me."

Dispatch asked, "Claude, what's your twenty?"

"East on three, just passed 140 Ave."

"East bound.......or west?"

"Yeah, east bound. He's still on my tail, trying to get my attention."

"Describe him."

"Brown; light brown, with a cow horns hood ornament."

"Cripes! Who's in the area?"

"Three's on it. Five miles away at his rear."

"Two, head on, seven miles."

"Claude has a fraud. Y'all be careful."

"I'm slowing down," Claude told dispatch. "Signalling to pull over; got a full load."

"Don't hurry to stop. Your help is not there yet."

Claude did take his time slowing down, but finally reported, "I'm stopped." He set the brakes. "Two of them are getting out of the car. Both of them have their pieces drawn, walking forward. Excuse me; gotta evade." Claude slipped into low, released his brakes and took off as best as his load would allow him. Finding second, he looked and saw that the guys had increased their pace and were at about mid-trailer. Third gear threw the load of cattle off their feet and onto the floor. At that time one of the guys turned back to get the car. The second one kept coming on the right, trying to find a handle to grab onto with his free hand, to pull himself up to the steps at the cab door. He might have made it too, had he not been carrying an extra hundred pounds around his middle and other places. He gave up trying, while Claude poured the cobs to range four. While waiting for a ride from the first guy, who had just gotten back to the car, the one caught sight of the lights of the approaching cars, both from the front and the rear. The car tires screamed as it bounded forward to pick up its passenger, who was standing beside the highway catching his breath. Its lights had been turned off.

While the brown car was stopped, loading up the passenger, the deputy in number one called. "Where you want me? I'm at east 90 Ave?"

Claude knew the area. "Tell him to pull south and go a mile to block off 50 St. I'm guessing my tail will go off on 110 to try to get away from your lights and sirens." Mabel did just that. "A mile south there's a curve to the east onto 50 St." Claude's right mirror shattered. "Made 'em mad. Just lost a rear mirror."

"Guys, they're armed and and using them." Mabel informed.

"10-4," one deputy said, and the other two clicked their mikes in acknowledgement.

"Claude's right," number three said. "They took off south. Man! He's haulin' balls! All I see is dust."

"Mabel, ya might as well call a meat wagon," Claude said. "There's a sharp dip down that road. He'll be airborne in about ten seconds, nine, eight, seven."

Deputy three was now in persuit down the dirt road.

"Don't make it two of you," Mabel said.

"……..four. He made it across! He jumped the whole dip and starting around the curve! Whoa! They slipped off into the south ditch. The passenger is kissing a barbed wire fence. The ditch is full of cattails; that'll stop them. Gators, guppies, and water puppies! They made it out, and back on the road going east."

"They're scared now," Mabel observed. "Number one, are you out of the way? Don't block the road. We don't need to buy a new car or a new driver."

"I'm back from the corner. A combine coming from the south……make that a swather."

"Stop the farmer!"

"No time. The guys saw my lights anyway and did a one-eighty; heading back west again."

Claude was still on the line with dispatch. "He's seen the road now," he said as he continued on down the highway with his load. "He knows what he has to do."

"What's that?"

"Hide the car, and take Shank's pony."

"Huh?"

"There use to be a driveway into an old homestead, and a tree grove between there and the river. They may try to lose you on foot; might just do it. Good luck." Claude shut his phone off and let the law do their job.

All the deputies met at the overgrown driveway. Jim, in number three, was told to watch out at the road while one and two drove through the weeds and young trees to the end of the long lane. It made no sense to Jim, because it was obvious that the brown car, or any other vehicle had not driven into that driveway for a long time.

"We lost 'em dispatch."

"How?"

"It had to be somewhere down 50. We'll try to back out of here and go look." Since there was no room to turn around, that was their only choice.

Claude's phone was ringing. How could he help them now? He was well on down the road and clear out of their area. It was Relda.

"Are you OK?"

"Yeah, why?"

"I felt the urge to pray for you. I did, until I got peace."

"Wow! You just had a direct connection to God!"

"Something did happen then?"

"'bout got shot or killed is all." He gave Relda a quick version of what had taken place and what was still ongoing. "I'll fill in the details when I get unloaded and back home. By then they might have caught the guys. And thanks! Love ya!"

The county deputies, now back out on the low-maintenance road, slowly drove the two mile stretch, turned around, then drove back west. Noticing an old sand pit and a small mountain of sand, they stopped to look behind it.

"I'm going to walk it," one said.

"I'll drive it." another added. "Jim, you watch the two cars and the road." Being the junior man on the force had once again elected him to be a parking attendant. The two deputies were gone about ten minutes, but they came back with a story.

"Looks like they drove in and hid, until we got down east, then they backed out and headed west and back north."

That almost sounded possible to Jim. It would only have worked if none of the three of them had looked back as they drove closer to the east intersection, but it was about a mile and a half. It was doable. But then again, number one had reported seeing the brown car close to him before it doubled back toward the sand pile, if that was even where they went. That was only moments before he, and number two a few minutes later, came down that same road.

Jim heard something, and told the other two. "I hear a car coming down 110." They listened for awhile then he continued. "No, it's going up 110." From where, he wondered?

Number one radioed dispatch, "We got skunked."

"Is it over?"

"Might as well be. We lost them. We were sure we had them surrounded. Guess they had a better plan."

"Are you leaving?" Jim asked.

"Do you see any reason to stay?" asked number two.

"I'm going to linger awhile to see if they come back."

"OK, Sherlock."

When the other two were gone, Jim took his own walk around the sand pile and pit. Quite a ways in, he found a large abandoned round top farm building. There were dead limbs strewn all around it, including in front of the large doors and the walk-in door. The large doors were secured from the inside, it appeared. The walk-in door was locked as well. The building had no windows or even a single crack that Jim could see into. He climbed over the debris all around the building and found nothing but thick growth of young trees, and more debris.

Back out to his car again, Jim drove over to the overgrown lane. He chose to walk the lane instead of getting stuff wrapped around his axles or drive shaft. He saw what Claude had described to dispatch: old buildings, which were unusable, and the growth of trees. As he turned to head back to his car, he heard a cow lowing. It sounded closer than the river. So he turned again and walked farther in, past the trees. What he saw there seemed unreal. There was a large pen of livestock, feeders with hay, two tanks with water, and even salt blocks. The brands on the cattle were many. The ear tags were colored various colors also. The pen did not have any loading capabilities, so that would have to be brought in, or the cattle driven to a place on the other side of the river for load out. How could the other two have missed that? The way he almost did, he presumed.

Getting back to his car, Jim looked at the time. It was past noon and his doughnut had long been digested. Just one more thing to look for, he told himself. Where had that car he heard earlier come from? Did it silently come from the highway, then head back to the highway making noise? The dip seemed a good place to start his search. Off to the east from the concrete bottomed dip was the creek that flowed over the road. It seemed to be eight to ten feet wide, and it beckoned Jim to have a look. He took off his shoes and waded the creek as it twisted from the north and again from the east. There he came face to face with a camouflaged tunnel. Throwing back some of the tree limbs at the end of the tunnel he saw an opening that was large enough to accommodate a small automobile. He proceeded to walk into the tunnel, being careful to not hit his six-foot-two head. Not far into the tunnel, there was a big door which was hinged at the top. The bottom of the door reached almost to the water in the creek. At that point, the creek was over a foot deep. Jim pulled on the door and found it to be securely fastened to something.

Jim thought for a moment, and having a bit of a detective nature, he returned to the mouth of the tunnel where he took off his LBE with his gun, radio, wallet, and sunglasses. Returning to the door, he knelt in the cold water and reached his arm under the door, finding that the depth of the water was consistent with the outside depth. Taking a deep breath, Jim went sideways under the door through the chilly creek water. He stood on the inside, finding it to be a continuation of what was outside. In the nearly pitch darkness, Jim felt his way along the wall and ceiling. After awhile he found a ramp, also concrete. Climbing the ramp, he hit head on the ceiling, but it was like a flat roof, and made of wood. Ahha! Jim suddenly knew where he was. He was under the floor of the big round top. What an ingenious escape setup!

Jim quickly but carefully made his way back out to the door, under the door, and after picking up his equipment, on out to his squad car. Feeling there was something yet undone, he remembered the limbs over the tunnel entrance. Oops, he almost blew his cover of having been in the area. Being meticulous to get the opening covered like he had found it, he gave himself a mental pat on the back and returned to the car. He picked up his boots but only carried them to the car where he got in, wet clothes and all.

Driving immediately to the Sheriff Office door, he rang in, and was let in by Mabel who stood speechless. Standing barefooted behind the Sheriff, the Sheriff turned in his chair to face him.

"Where have you been!"

"At the scene of the crime."

"Have a seat! This I want to hear!"

The Sheriff turned on his recorder, closed his inner-office door, and placed the mike in front of his junior officer. Soon Jim had painted the whole picture.

"Get into some dry clothes. This I gotta see for myself." While Jim was changing, the Sheriff got an old unclaimed pickup out of the pound. He and Jim loaded up and rode out of town. Jim, I'm going to give you two days paid leave, starting at near dark tonight."

"It might take longer than that to recover from pneumonia." The Sheriff chuckled. "Did I do something wrong?"

"Hardly. You and I are going to solve this case. No one else can know. No one!"

"Do you think one of our guys are in on this?"

"No, I would guess they both are. You and I will have to prove it."

"How?"

"In the back I have surveillance cameras and a recorder. We'll set them up before dark. You will get some sleep, then watch the monitor until daylight. Are you up to that?"

"Sure!"

The set-up was made and at ten o'clock Jim drove

the old pickup back out to a hidden location. There he connected the two leads that came from the cameras. He covered the pickup with camouflage, sprayed his exposed skin with insect repellant, and called the office phone.

"I'm set," he told Mabel.

"I'll tell him," she said. "You got good pictures?"

"Yeah," Jim almost whispered. "Bye for now."

"God bless."

"Thanks." While he waited, looking at the green monitor, Jim recalled his story he told the Sheriff. How could one vehicle evade three officers without a little help under the table? Why were they clustered into a small location instead of branching out? Had deputy one not actually seen the brown car up close, if at all? Was there really a combine or swather, or not? Why was number two taking so long to join in the search? It doesn't take fifteen minutes to drive six miles. Where did the brown car go after it slung mud and cattails getting out of the ditch? Would it not be helpful if the tunnel had already been uncovered for a quick excape? He would have seen the brown car coming back from two miles east before it got to the sand pile. No, he did not see a combine or swather. No, he did not get to see what the others saw while they were looking, and it shouldn't take twenty-five minutes to look around a round top; maybe fifteen.

Nothing showed on the monitor all night. Jim unhooked, went home and then drove his own car to the Sheriff's office at the time deputies one and two had come to work. He got his crutches out of his car and favored his left foot as he entered the office.

"Sherlock! Did you find the bad guys?"

"Found a badger hole."

"And you came to work like that?"

"I'll be all right in a couple of days, you'll see."

"You been here long enough for comp?"

"Cut it out! It's not funny. Tell the Sheriff I'll be in tomorrow morning. I'm going home." Jim left and met the Sheriff in the parking lot.

"Oh, no! What happened?"

"Sheriff, it's all fake. I'm due another nap. Got some late night duty tonight. I think tonight's the night."

"I think you are right. I'll catch some Z's and be out and about tonight too. Here is my cell number."

"I'll program it into mine, so I wouldn't forget it."

"When we are done, please erase it. OK?"

"I will."

"Jim, help is on the way, in case you think you and I are it, and that is all I will say about that now."

"Thanks for reassuring me with that much." Jim went on home and did get a meal, a shower, and a big nap. His squad car was at the office location. The pickup that he would use again tonight was in his garage.

"Super snoop got himself hurt," one of the deputies told the other. "Can we get along without him for a couple of days?"

"We got along without him before we met him; we can get along without him now," one sang. Both Mabel and the Sheriff heard.

"Sounds like bullying."

"Doesn't it though. I'd watch those two."

"Why?"

"They are too cocky."

"You noticed that too? I will."

The Sheriff had called Steven Serpa the evening before Jim started surveillance. Steve, with the help from three more ranches, drove the stolen cattle to other secure locations. There were over three hundred head. The gate to the big pen was left open only enough to make it appear that the cattle had broken through and wandered away. Not likely would 911 be called to report those missing cattle.

Jim got set up on the second evening just before dark, and not too soon. A compact convertible came down 110 Ave, turned at the dip, drove up the creek bed and then stopped at the entrance to the tunnel. The big guy was not among the passengers. Two of them were very familiar to Jim. The cameras and the recorder got a good picture of each of them.

The branches were quickly cleared, making the opening fully usable. The big door in the tunnel swang upward on its hinges. The three got back into the compact and it disappeared into the tunnel. The big door came down behind them. All was quiet for awhile as if the show was over.

No camera was set up out on 50 St where a car-hauling truck pulled to a stop near the sand pit, turned around, and stopped again, headed back east. Its long bed proceeded to tilt. Jim could see it from his hiding place. He turned on the recorder for the camera at the doors of the round top. The little door came open first, followed by three guys coming out who cleared the dead branches away from the approach to the big doors. Communication could be heard from one of them to the truck driver.

"Are you ready to load?"……………….. "OK, we're backing out now." The doors to the big shed separated and the brown car, minus the hood ornament and lights, backed out. It turned around and was driven along the edge of the sand pit and around the sand pile to the waiting truck. The small car came out also, but not all the way to the truck. Loading took only about two minutes. By the time the bed was lowered, the tarp was being fastened to the truck.

"They are coming for the cattle tomorrow morning for Omaha. Payday is next week. We did good! No, we did BAD."

"Omaha? Why so far away?"

"Cause that's where the packers are, stupid!"

"I'm going with the big guy in the truck. That back seat in the bug is way too cramped."

"Time's a wastin', go!" The compact with two passengers went back to the building.

No, it didn't take long, but long enough for the Federal Marshall to set up a seal at the east end of 50 St and at the intersection of 110 Ave and the highway.

Jim hadn't been on the force very long, but he was, according to the Sheriff, due a promotion. Is anybody qualified to fill the other two positions? All applicants will be considered. Until then, unit one and unit two will sit unused beside the Sheriff's Office.

Chapter thirty
Who and Why?"

At church one winter Sunday, Effie found herself looking at everyone's facial expressions and also trying to catch someone looking at her. She found no one looking any different than they had always looked. What was she looking for? She was trying to detect who might have been responsible for her new pile of firewood next to her house. Getting down to what would have kept her warm for only a week or two, she was hoping for a warm still day that she could go looking for more, to keep her warm a little longer. She did not have any money available to buy some already cut and she for sure did not want to beg for any. Over night a whisper of snow had fallen which had covered any automobile tracks in her driveway. The ground was frozen, so there would be no mud tracks. Her neighbors, out there in the country were so far away that they would not have noticed who could have done it. The stack wasn't so large that she would not need more later on, but it would be near spring before what she now had would be gone. God had been good to her and had used one of his children to carry out the good deed.

Sam had had a similar experience, and he did voice his discovery during Sunday School. A tire on his old pickup, his only transportation, had gotten down to where cords were showing, and he often had to put air in it to keep it from going flat. After noticing that he no longer was having to do that, he looked closer, discovering that the tire had some pretty good tread on it still. It was not a new tire, but obviously someone had replaced the bad one with a much better one. The only time that could have taken place would have been while he was drinking coffee with the men at the Coop some week day morning. Could it have been one of the Coop workers who had done that? No one came forward admitting to the deed.

Ed, the owner of the local cafe, had instructed his helpers to put carrot and potato peelings into a bucket separate from the other scraps and trash. Nobody questioned him for his reason. At the edge of town was a lady who raised a few laying hens. She had noticed that her egg production had not faltered like it always had before when the colder weather came. Her order for eggs to be delivered to the café each week could be fully supplied by her own chickens. Ed never divulged what he had done with the peelings each day, but he stepped out at near ten each morning.taking the peelings with him, and bringing back an empty bucket.

Similar things were happening all over the community. Who was responsible for each of them or all of them was yet to be discovered. A few knew the answer to some of the secrets, but they were sworn to not tell. It was almost like there was a competition to see who could do the most without getting caught. When anyone helped anyone else, whether it was known or unknown, they might have been returning favors to someone who had helped them.

Chapter thirty-one
Church Visitor

Just as the last song was being sung before the sermon was to be preached, Pastor Mark went to his study for a moment. He was gone for only a minute or so, returning before the song had finished. He sat in his big chair, singing with the congregation. As the last notes were being played, a figure appeared at the entrance to the sanctuary behind the pews.

Immediately Mark rose to his feet, and after the song, greeted the visitor. The late arriver had on a long chore coat and a plain towel, held on his head by a band above his eyebrows circling his head.

"Welcome!" Mark said. "We are honored to have you worship with us this morning. Would you like to introduce yourself, and are you alone?"

"It is just me, today. I am Ruben. I have come with a message, if I might, at this Christmas time."

"Is it a Christmas message?"

"It definitely is. It is not foreign to what you read,

sing and speak about each Christmas. I would say that it is my testimony."

"Then I would say, come up here to the microphone. We are grateful for testimonies." The guest was not shy, but after shaking hands with Mark, turned to stand at the microphone."

"Thank you for your warm welcome. As I said, my name is Ruben. My last name would be hard for you to pronounce. My testimony starts when I was twelve years old. My father had asked me to join him for one night while he did his appointed duty guarding a large flock of sheep on the Bethlehem hillside. The flock did not belong to my father, and the watching of them was shared by several. Oh, it was a special flock. The sheep were all pure white; not a black spot on any of them. Also, no blemish of any kind could be found on even one of them. One of the shepherds' daily chores was to inspect the sheep, mostly by close observation, to look for flaws of any sort. Some flocks were not that cared for; in fact I would guess that very few were. Each sheep in this flock was hand picked to be used for the animal sacrifices in the Temple. Sheep used for that purpose were to be pure. The reason being, as my father had informed me, was that there was coming a Savior who would be offered as a sacrifice for the people; not just for our people, but for all people. I had no clue why that had to be, but I assumed that it was a lesson I was yet to learn.

I did not have to stand on my feet all night, but wherever my father was, on the circle around the flock, there I was also. The sheep at that time of the night were resting, ruminating on what they had eaten during the grazing hours. We boys were instructed on what we should believe and what the reasons were to believe it. At the moment there were no distractions. We were not to be sleeping because the animal preditors use the darkness of night to choose a sheep or lamb to be its next meal. Straying animals had all been rescued and accounted for by sunset. My father told me that people often stray; just wanting to do their own thing, and getting in trouble needing rescued by somebody. Those sheep who were trouble makers were ostracized or slightly injured to bring them back to submission. Don't we bring injury on ourselves by doing or saying what we ought not? Even when we are forgiven, we may still carry the scars that remind us of our errors.

By now, you may be starting to be bored by my message. I was getting bored that night myself, but then all of a sudden, the near pitch darkness became as bright as the noonday sun. We all sprang to our feet, not knowing what was happening or why. We wanted to hide or run, forgetting our mission to watch the sheep. Then appeared the Angel of the Lord saying, "Fear not; for behold, I bring you good tidings of great joy, which shall be to all people. For unto you is born this day in the city of David, a Savior, which is Christ the Lord. And this shall be a sign unto you; you shall find the babe wrapped in swaddling clothes, lying in a manger. And just as quickly there was with the angel a whole bunch of angels praising God and saying, 'Glory to God in the highest, and on earth peace, good will toward men.'

Wow! What a thing for a twelve-year-old to witness! The angels soon went back into the heavens, and the shepherds immediately began talking about going down to Bethlehem to see what the angel was telling them had happened. I went with my father, hurrying to Bethlehem to see what the angel had told us we would find. It didn't take long. We found the manger, which had been where animal feed had been placed for the animals to eat. The baby lay in the manger, wrapped in swaddling clothes, just as the angel had said. Mary and Joseph were there with their baby. Who would believe it? That did not stop us from telling it to anyone who would listen and even to those who did not believe a word of our experience. People were amazed to hear what we told them.

Mary and Joseph stayed in Bethlehem with their baby. No, they did not make the stable or cave their new home. In fact, a year or so later a few of what was called the Maji came on camels as the book of Isaiah said they would. By then the little family was in a house. The kings from the East opened gifts and presented them to the young child. There was gold and frankincense and myrrh, expensive gifts. They said that they had seen His star in the East and come to Jerusalem, then followed the star to Bethlehem. The kings' visit was cut short because an angel had warned them in a dream to now return to their far-away homes without telling king Herod where they had found the baby who was to be a new king for the Jews.

King Herod was wroth when he heard that the kings from the East had not returned to tell him about the baby. So he sent soldiers to kill all the boy babies who were less than two years old. He did not want anyone of any age to take his place on the throne as a ruler of the Jews

Joseph was also warned in a dream to immediately leave Bethlehem because, as the angel said, Herod was seeking to kill Jesus. Joseph took his wife, Mary, and Jesus and left Bethlehem by night escaping into Egypt until they received word that Herod was dead.

Nazareth was where Jesus grew into manhood. He had gone to Jerusalem at the same age I was when I started watching sheep. He later taught people about God and what God wanted from His people; and He himself was God. At about the age of thirty-three, Jesus was tried, and then hung on a cross where he died. Three days later, He arose from the tomb. Forty days after that He took some of his followers and went out into the country where they witnessed his ascending into Heaven. The good news is, that He is coming back to get us, that where He is, there we will be, not just for a period of time, but for eternity. Thank you for hearing my story. I must be on my way. God bless you all."

The gentleman walked right on out through the big doors and, as such, was not seen again.

Pastor Mark stood before the mike, "All we, like sheep, have gone astray; everyone has turned to his own way. The Lord hath laid on Him the iniquity of us all. It would have been good if Randy had been here. He would have enjoyed that." Ben and Becky faced each other and both winked. Some of the children often looked toward the doors until the service was over.

Chapter thirty-two
White-out

Those who live in the northern third of the United States forty-eight states and notably those whose livelihoods depend on driving the roads of America, shudder when they encounter the condition of white-out. Bobby was a rural letter carrier and on one of those days when the snow seemed to be coming down horizontally, he still had to get in his pickup and drive to the post office. After that he was assigned to deliver all the mail to all of the customers on his route that he could get to under those conditions.

"Be careful," Karen said as her man finished pulling his winter hat over his head. In one way it sounded like an order. Bobby was certain that he didn't need to be reminded of such things, yet he almost expected to hear the word "please!"

"I will," Bobby told her, then added, "Please pray." He didn't know if his wife prayed for him or not. In case she needed reminded, this was certainly a good time, he supposed.

He took a mental inventory of the things he had in his truck as he closed the front door of his house. He took another look at the house as he opened the truck's driver's door. Karen was looking out the window. She did care!

As Bobby rounded the corner of his farm shop, he thought of his winch that he had purchased over two years ago. He had attached the winch to an A frame that could either be used with a ball hitch or an ordinary draw bar, and extended the wiring so that it could reach the vehicle's battery. From the stuff Bobby stored in the bed of his pickup, the word overkill would come to mind. A large tow rope, as well as a twenty foot log chain, a clevis and three different sizes of hitch pins lay over and under jacks, lug wrenches, and a spare tire.

With all of that loaded, Bobby headed down the road toward the post office. His six-days-a- week mail route would be more than routine today. The air temperature was in the mid twenties. The snow had been falling all night and the wind was surely above forty miles per hour. Actually the snow did not appear to be falling at all. The wind kept some spots swept clean and piled it up extra deep in other places. The early morning darkness only added to the hazard of not being able to see much of the road ahead.

Suddenly Bobby let up on the gas pedal before he detected a reason to. In his outside mirror he caught a glimpse of an angus cow as she made her way across the road behind him. Why hadn't he seen it before? It had to be because the left side of the cow was totally snow covered. Were there more?

That question was answered in a heartbeat. One was lying at the edge of the highway. Pulling over and stopping, Bobby got out of the pickup and walked back to the lying animal. It had been hit and was now unable to stand because of broken legs. If only he had been allowed to carry his gun with him on his job, he could stop the animal's pain. As it was, he couldn't.

A call to 911 to report the straying livestock would probably be his next move. It wasn't however, because he distinctly heard a call for help. Looking on the left side of the road, Bobby saw the white top of a vehicle almost completely out of sight in the big ditch. He walked down to it. The driver quickly told Bobby about his dilemma.

"I can't get any traction to make it back up to the road."

"Is your car drivable?"

"Yeah. I may be high centered too."

"You didn't hit the cow?"

"No. I swerved to miss another one, and got myself in this mess."

"I think I can get you out," Bobby told him. Stay with your car. Do you have passengers?"

"My family."

"Are they all right?"

"A couple of them bumped their heads and are crying. They are more scared than hurt."

Bobby called 911 when he got back to his truck. "They are probably Marshall Blackwell's cattle."

"We'll call them," the dispatcher told him.

"I think I can winch out the car," Bobby volunteered. "Do you have an officer available to send out?"

"They are all tied up at the moment with other accidents. Don't risk making matters worse, Bobby. You are Bobby aren't you?"

"I am, and I will be careful." That was now the second time he had tried to reassure someone today. He told the dispatcher his location. Bobby pulled out his log chain and drug one end of it down to the car, losing his balance and falling on the embankment. His shoulder took the brunt of the fall, but the injury was minimal and he would continue his mission. Lying on the snow at the rear of the car which was nose down in the ditch. Bobby found a spring shackle and fastened the chain around it. He couldn't reach the axle, and even if he could have, there was always the chance of rupturing a brake line.

The chain reached the edge of the roadway. He might be able to attach the winch cable to it. He dared not be on the traveling lanes lest blinded drivers run into his pickup or the tightened cable. Then he attached the winch onto the pickup ball. It seemed to take forever to get all that done; and would you believe, the cable lacked five feet of reaching the log chain.

Pulling out the tow rope, Bobby laid it out, attaching it to the outstretched cable and then to the shortened chain. Opening the truck hood and attaching the electric cables to the truck battery, Bobby prepared to reel in the slack cable and then to pull out the car. His fingers were getting increasingly colder as he got the cable tightened, but he couldn't stop now.

Then came the awful sound: A vehicle was approaching them and it couldn't be seen through the storm. Bobby quickly reversed the winch and allowed the cable to go slack, stepping on it just as a semi breezed past them over the rope and the cable.

"Thank you, Jesus," Bobby prayed. "My plan isn't working. Let's go with yours." Bobby walked carefully back to the stranded car and explained to the man about the situation and the near mishap with the lifted cable and the semi. "The way I see it, we had probably better just take you to my house and wait until the wind goes down to retrieve your car.

"All right."

"There is only one other alternative as I see it."

"What's that?"

"I could hook my truck directly to the tow rope and take off down the road like you weren't there behind me, essentially yanking you out."

"I've seen that work. Let's do it"

"I'll hook up and yell go when I am ready. Everybody buckle up."

"God bless us all."

Bobby unhooked the winch cable and reeled it in. He took the winch off, placing it back into the bed of the pickup. He lined the truck up on the side of the road that the car was on, not yet putting it out into the driving lanes. His phone was ringing.

"Hello!"

"Are you hung up?" It was the postmaster.

"I'm not. Someone else is. I'm trying to get him out."

"Good! No mail has gotten to the post office yet, and it won't be here before noon, if then. If you want, just go home, and we'll try again tomorrow."

"Boy! I am glad to hear you say that. It takes a little of the stress off."

"Good luck with the pull-out."

"Don't need it. We are using God's plan now."

"Wish I had your faith."

"Mine isn't much. We are using Jesus' faith now."

"Huh?"

"I will explain it to you some day."

"Please! Goodbye."

Bobby walked down to the car. The man opened the window.

"Ready?"

"I'll yell GO!"

"OK! Jesus you're on." said Andy.

"For sure," Bobby agreed. He walked back up to his truck, nearly falling again. He seated himself and powered down the right window. "Ready, GO!" Bobby put the pedal to the metal while nosing his truck out onto the driving lanes. His truck came to a sudden stop, then lurched forward again as the tow rope was doing its thing. Two more lurches and then the pull-out was complete. Bobby pulled back over to the emergency lane, and started unhitching from the car. Another car was pulling up behind them. Lights were flashing all over the place. It's driver congratulated Bobby for a job well done.

"How did you get traction on this ice?" he asked.

"God did it," Bobby told him.

"Are you sure?" the patrolman asked

"You figure it out, if you can," Bobby said. "There is no other way."

"Could be," he said as he walked away shaking his head.

"Could be?" Andy, from the white car said. He and Bobby laughed triumphantly, giving each other a brotherly hug.

"We are closing this road," the officer said as he reemerged from his car for as long as it took to say it. Bobby and his new friend waved acknowledgement. The patrolman turned his car around and headed it toward town.

"How far did you need to go yet?"

"Too far," Andy said.

"Follow me to my house."

"Sounds good, if I can turn this thing around."

A farm tractor pulled to a stop beside the downed cow. Bobby approached him on foot.

"Semi got her," the cow owner said. You want her? I have another one on down the road."

"Sure! Can you load her in my truck?"

"I'll bleed her and do that."

"I'll help you when we get to your house," Andy volunteered. "I do butchering."

"I'll share it with you." The young cow was soon loaded and Andy had gotten his car turned around. He followed Bobby home.

Bobby called Karen and told her the short version, informing her of the coming guests.

"Hot chocolate will be waiting," she said.

"Praise God!"

"Praise God!" Karen echoed.

Chapter thirty-three
The KBC

It was the weekend after thanksgiving and the Reeds were enjoying the evening in front of the fireplace. Daniel was being self entertained with some of his toys. Ben and Becky were having the time of their life watching their son, no TV necessary. It has been said that perfect evenings can be too perfect. That was true for two families recently when they were murdered at their homes by robbers in the night. So, when the front gate buzzer sounded, both Ben and his wife were startled.

"Just in case this is not good," Ben said, "Let's prepare like we have practiced." Becky took Daniel into the back bedroom. She locked and double barred the door. Turning on only a small light and then checking her cell phone, she waited. Ben had, by then, sent the signal that unlocked and opened the gate. He turned off the kitchen lights and stood watching out the window that lined up with the driveway. A single car was starting up the lane. It wasn't coming particularly fast but neither was it creeping in. The yard light revealed a white or off-white sedan. Ben switched windows as the car pulled on around to the front door area. His revolver was on a locked shelf nearby. Seeing two adults and two children climb out of the car was enough to show Ben that he had nothing to dread, whatsoever. He left his gun on the locked shelf and opened the front door for his visitors.

"Come right on in!" he greeted. "Take off your coats and find a seat." While they did that, Ben walked down the hall and planted a knocking code on the bedroom door. Becky completed the signal from her side and started unlocking the barred door. Returning to the living room, where the visitors were finishing their coat removal, Ben realized who they were. He had not recognized them sooner because they were so bundled up in their winter coats, until they got inside the house.

As Becky and Daniel entered the living room, Ben introduced them to her.

"Becky, Mr. and Mrs. Windom and their children." Turning to them and continuing, "My wife and Daniel."

When Hellos were through, Becky announced, "The hot chocolate will soon be ready," and turned to the kitchen. Daniel followed his mother.

"This is a much nicer evening than when we first met," Ben stated, to start a conversation.

Mrs. Windom was quick to tell her feelings about that. "A part of me wants to forget that experience, and yet I want to cherish it forever, thanks to you."

Mr. Windom made his offering, "I wasn't sure you were for real. I would just as easily believed that you were an angel, ushering me and us all to paradise."

"God did have a large part in your rescue, you know." Ben said. Becky then knew that they were the ones that Ben had found in the snow storm. She entered the room with the hot chocolate.

"We know that quite well. One reason we came tonight is because we have a name for you and we wanted to share this with you. Oh, by the way; I am Maxwell and this is Marteena. Our two girls are Sheri and Shawna."

"Here are some marshmallows and some spoons," Becky announced. After pouring the hot chocolate and passing the marshmallows, Becky wanted to know, "What have you renamed my man?"

Maxwell spoke up. "My wife made our adventure into a short-story poem. Did you bring it, sweetheart?"

"Yes. Here it is." She started to hand it to Ben.

Becky asked, "Could you read it to us, to help us get your full feelings?"

"If you want me to." Marteena unfolded the page after she had set her cup on the coffee table. "At first I tried to make it a poem......had to give that up, for the most part. Some of it still rhymes." She began to read: "We had a late Thanksgiving, with Mama and my Dad. We knew we had stayed long enough, the weather was turning bad. At first we didn't know it was snowing; just that the wind was picking up. We probably would have waited, but we thought about our pup. We'd left it out in the yard, and thought it would be all right. The weather man had missed his guess; this storm was now a fright. So we started out, heading south. We lived four hours away. We hoped it would get better; it would, but not today. In fact it got worse and worse, and then we got on ice. How many circles we made on that bridge, was it more than twice? When we got stopped, we eased on out, for the last hour of the trip. We were being much more careful now; didn't want another slip. Our driveway didn't look at all the same, all covered up with snow. We pulled off the road and into it, and kept on going slow. Where is our house? That's not our house! We must be at someone else's place. Let's ask someone just where we are and how far we've yet to drive. We found a place to turn around and then somehow got stuck. "You guys stay here," Max said. I'll walk back to the road and I'll flag down a truck. We had one blanket for us three. It was really not enough. I woke up when at my window I heard a little knock. A man gave us a sleeping bag and I looked at the clock. It was nearing three A.M., and we might be far from home, yet with the sleeping bag for the girls I knew we would get warm. Max, we heard, had gotten lost: The main road was the other way. There was nothing we could do; nothing that is, but pray. The stranger had found Maxwell and used his own body to warm him up that night. An ambulance came at daylight and took our Max away. The stranger came back to our car and carried each girl to his truck, then helped me get there through the deep snow. He took us to the hospital where we joined Max. He was doing well. A day later another person took us back to our car, which had been pulled out, refueled and readied for the road. We must have gotten turned around on that slick bridge and headed back the way we had come. Our dog was all right. The weather had warmed a bit by then.

Until just recently we didn't know who rescued us and probably saved our lives, and to us, Mr. Reed…you are 'The Knight before Christmas.'"

"That's beautiful!" Becky exclaimed.

"Isn't it though!" Ben agreed. "Hey! It's not stormy tonight. How about singing some Christmas songs?"

The guests enthusiastically agreed. Ben got his guitar.

Chapter thirty-four
Bearcats

The winter was plenty cold and snowy, but probably not as bad as the record-breaking year before. Daniel and Grace had both sent and received two letters from each other. Daniel was open with his; Grace had privately given hers from Daniel to her daddy to put with the first one.

Sharon had resolved to wait until the time when her daughter wanted to share, if that day ever came at all.

As the nicer days of Spring peeked into the end of Winter, Becky was looking forward to escaping from the four walls that she enjoyed with her family all winter.

"It has been a long time since I visited Relda," Becky told Ben one evening. "I hope she is still improving."

"Then I suppose you are going to find out?" He knew his wife well enough to know that she would not voice a thought without finding an answer.

"I'm thinking I had better. Don't want her thinking, 'Out of sight, out of mind.' She may not be beyond an emotional relapse."

"Are you planning a surprise visit?"

"I wouldn't want anyone to do that to me, so no, I had better call her now." She did.

Relda's phone rang five times before she answered. "Hello, who is this?"

"Hi Relda. This is Becky. How ya doin'?"

"Oh, so-so."

"I've been thinking about you, for all the good that does. Care if I stop by tomorrow to visit?"

"If you want to. I'm not very entertaining."

"Would eight be too early?"

"I'd probably look like a scarecrow, but if that won't scare you, eight would be fine."

"Well, OK then."

"I have a couple of questions saved up for when we got together again," Relda said.

"Not hard ones, I hope."

"I doubt if they are for you."

"Now don't build me up. I might disappoint you."

"You don't drink coffee, do you?"

"No, I really don't."

"I thought I remembered that."

"I guess we can't pick and choose what we remember and what we try to forget."

"You said a mouthful there. If you can't make it, I will understand."

"I will call if I am unable. See you then."

Becky opted not to take her Bible or other Bible helps with her. In case Relda's questions were beyond her memorized answers. Supposing that there would be other times where they could study in depth, she would allow herself the privilege of not knowing everything at this visit. God was still the provider of the wisdom and the timing.

One thing Becky was a stickler about, was punctuality. At eight A.M. she was standing at Relda's front door, pushing the doorbell button. The door came open immediately as if Relda were waiting on the other side with her hand on the knob. She was not all frazzled, but well combed and well clothed.

"Do come in! What a beautiful day."

"Isn't it!"

"You didn't bring Daniel?"

"He's helping Daddy this morning."

"Watching the trees grow?"

"No. He said that he and Daddy were going hunting bearcats, whatever that is." Both of the ladies chuckled.

"I was going to guess that it was skunks," Relda offered. "But I guess that would be polecats."

Becky made a face. "I cringe to even think about it. I don't have enough tomato juice to give them both a bath."

"I thought that was tomato soup."

"We might have a few cans of that."

"Are you ready for my questions?"

"Lay one out, and we'll take a look at it."

"What does God do with our sins when we confess them?"

"That one I know. He sends them as far away as the east is from the west."

"Not north or south?"

"I guess there is a limit to how far north or south they can go. That would mean that we could run into them again. He has no limits to His forgiveness. We never run out of east or west."

"Where can I read that?"

"I will have to look that up, unless you or Claude has a big concordance."

"Let me call him. I would guess that he does." Relda proceeded to do just that, and after he directed her to his bedside book shelf, she found the large book and brought it into her living room. "What do I look for?"

"Look for east or west." Relda looked up west and found the scripture that included the words 'east is from the west'." Then she took her Bible, now without the dust, and found the verses she was looking for. Getting a piece of printer paper, she jotted down the verses and where she had found them.

"That's good to know."

"For sure!" Becky agreed.

"My next question is one that probably no one this side of heaven knows."

"That includes me."

"Do you want to try?"

"Since it is just you and me, sure; why not?"

Relda began this way: "Noah and his wife were on the ark as well as the six others. Did Noah's parents and maybe grandparents all drown?"

"You are right. I don't know that answer, but Ben told me that the men's Bible study tackled genealogies a while back. I know it's a big question, but may I call Ben for that?"

"Certainly. If it is possible to know, I would like to."

Becky dialed Ben. "Hello."

"Ben, Relda and I want to know where the generations before the flood is found; the genealogies."

"Wow! You two jump in with both feet."

"Sometimes we learn to swim that way."

"Genesis, chapter five."

"All right! Thanks. You catch any bearcats yet?"

"We saw some hair on a tree branch. That may be as close as we get."

"Keep looking behind you. They may be hunting you while you hunt them."

Becky told Relda Ben's answer. Relda found chapter five quickly. The two started totaling the years, and by the time their visit was over, they had found out several things. They found that Noah's father died before his grandfather. His grandfather was Methuselah who lived to the age of nine hundred sixty-nine. Methuselah was a godly man. He died the year of the flood, but not in the flood. Adam, who died at age nine hundred thirty, only lacked a few years of seeing the birth of Noah. All the years from the beginning of creation until the flood and to the death of Noah were also added to the knowledge of the two ladies.

"We did it!" Becky cheered.

"We did it!" Relda echoed.

"Relda, this was fun! Save up some more questions and we'll try this again."

"Don't wait until I have questions. Just call to see if I am home, then come, anytime."

"Sounds good. Now I had better go home to see if we are having bearcats for supper or if I need to raid the freezer again."

"Could I offer a parting prayer before you go?"

Becky was delighted, "Please!!"

Chapter thirty-five
Centennial

For over a year the larger community of Butte had been in the planning stages of their town's centennial celebration. For three days June 1 through June 3, the folks in and near Butte were to bring their memories to share. Old pictures with short stories that went with them were coveted.

Some of the activities to be included were sandpit volleyball, horseshoe throwing, croquet, and softball games. These were to be scheduled on day one and two. Also on day one was to be homemade crafts shows and sales. The high school band would play a few patriotic songs. A parade of floats and a trail of old equipment and cars were expected. Of course the Prairie Schooners would be present with their covered wagons and carts. The children could compete in hoop rolling contests and stilt walking. The stilts were to be between six inches and two feet off the ground. Centennial hats, t-shirts, and banners were to be sold to help offset the cost of celebration expenses. Any leftover money was to be divided among needy families and/or businesses as the Mayor and city council saw fit.

On the second evening a block of main street would be roped off to any vehicle traffic. A farm truck would be used as a stage for those who wanted to speak about the times they remember most in their lifetime. Also a potluck picnic would be eaten at noon while visiting friends, relatives and neighbors.

On the third day, the cowgirls could show their skills in barrrel racing for as many as would sign up for the event. The men would bring their expertise in ranching skills in events of calf roping, bulldogging, cutting horse contests, bareback bronc, and bull riding. Rodeo entertainment was to be provided by a clown and a fellow with his trained buffalo.

The food vendors throughout the three-day celebration were the family cooks in the county. State and US franchises were not to be selling at this grand occasion.

It was a joy to watch young and old display their favorite things: singing, musical instrument playing, contest skills and almost any other new idea. Those events which were forbidden were the ones in which the contestants would harm the well-being of their opponents, such as boxing, wrestling, and any other form of fighting with or without weapons.

As the third day morning drew the crowds, the rodeo was being arranged so as to leave little time between events. Goat roping and mutton busting began that event. The ladies came next with their horseback skills. The area cattlemen would finish the rodeo events revealing who was the best on this particular day.

Finally it came time for the bull riding. Eight bulls had been shipped in by a rodeo stock provider, since none of the nearby ranches kept stock for that purpose. The first bull was named Windmill Sunday. The second was called Never, and no one had yet stayed on it for eight seconds. Third was called The School Teacher. It had taught many a cowboy a hard lesson. The fourth was Prairie Tornado. It tried to destroy the rider and anything else in its path. The fifth was called The Equalizer. The sixth, called Goliath, bellowed before, during and after it unloaded the rider. The seventh, Hop-along, did not do so much spinning as it did just jump up and down in the same spot. The eighth bull was saved especially for the last ride because of its skills and also its fierceness. It had been renamed in its history or rodeoing. It started out being World War I. Later it became World War II. The advertisement stated that this Bull had one thing in mind, to become World War III. As much as was required of any bull rider, to attempt this ride, he had to be skillful and a bit stupid, The one who chose World War II must surely not have a brain left in his head.

Behind the gate, World War II snorted so fiercely that the crowd imagined they could feel his hot breath from where they sat. Finally all the rigging was in place. The brave cowboy lowered himself onto the huge animal's back. Taking his free hand, he wrapped the rigging rope around his gloved hand as tightly as he could stand, and then he gave it another tug to be sure. He looked around to see if he could see any guardian angels. He didn't. He gave his head a toss and the keeper of the gate pulled the latch and swung the gate all the way open. World War II charged into the arena bucking all the way. He circled and bucked, then twisted the other way while doing more of the same. The cowboy stayed as tight to the animal as he could. At eight seconds, the buzzer screamed. The rider tried to get loose from the rope in his hand. Someone must have applied super glue, because he was bound to it. The crowd drew silent. The bull did not slow down its twisting or its bucking. It charged farther and farther into the open arena. The clown was trying to catch up in case he was needed to protect the rider once he was thrown off the devilish beast.

Steve instinctly mounted Bessie and demanded a gate be opened to allow him into the arena. He spurred Bessie as close to the ferocious animal as he could get. As soon as the rider could get loose, Steve would attempt to snatch him away and to safety. The bull saw Steve and his mare. Not stopping its twisting, snorting, or bucking, it charged into Bessie, throwing both the mare and Steve across the arena.

Watching all this take place, Ben felt utterly helpless. Suddenly finding himself holding a deer rifle which had been thrust into his hands by a rodeo stock company man, he heard a voice shouting, "Kill him! He's mine! Kill Him!!" Ben knew he had no time to look at ownership papers; he braced himself against an arena post, found the side of the charging bull's head in his scope, and just as he pulled the trigger, Steve was also in his round picture, at the nose of the bull.

B A N G !! At the last tenth of a second, Steve rolled his body to his left. The bull charged on by. It's rider, finally loose from the rigging, and flung onto the ground, got to his feet and limped toward the far fence. Steve gave a whistle. Bessie heard, rose to her feet, and at full gallop, charged toward her master. Steve swung himself into the saddle without using the stirrups and reined Bessie toward the limping bull rider. As he came alongside the bull rider he reached out his left arm preparing to lean to his right. The bull rider grabbed Steve's arm with both hands and swung onto Bessie behind Steve.

Before Bessie could get moving again, there came World War II. Ben was ready to make his second pull on the trigger when suddenly World War II's knees buckled and its head became a plow, opening a furrow in the floor of the arena. The first shot had been good. It had taken a few seconds for it to take effect. The next stop for World War II would be the butcher shop. The hamburger, no doubt, would have to be double ground. World War III was avoided, thank God!

Who was the rodeo hero? This was the community of Butte; so as always, GOD was. The men should be given an A+ for following their hearts to be their brothers' keepers. This celebration would be often spoken of and for a long time.

NOT EVERYONE THAT SAITH UNTO ME, LORD, LORD SHALL ENTER INTO THE KINGDOM OF HEAVEN; BUT HE THAT DOETH THE WILL OF THE FATHER WHICH IS IN HEAVEN. ENTER YE IN AT THE STRAIT GATE: FOR WIDE IS THE GATE, AND BROAD IS THE WAY WHICH LEADETH TO DESTRUCTION, AND MANY THERE BE WHICH TRY TO GO IN THEREAT: BECAUSE STRAIT IS THE GATE, AND NARROW IS THE WAY WHICH LEADETH UNTO ETERNAL LIFE, AND FEW THERE BE THAT FIND IT. GREATER LOVE HATH NO MAN THAN THAT HE LAY DOWN HIS LIFE FOR A FRIEND.

About The Author

Lowell Gridley was born and raised on farms. He was familiar with 'fixing' something so that it works or else making something that is even better.

Recently, he retired from over thirty-two years of working as a (rural) letter carrier. Also, in his past, he served over thirty years of military duty. Road maintenance, School bus driving, welding, barn building and farming are included in his experiences.

One of his favorite sayings is: "There has got to be a way…"

About eternity, Lowell knows that Jesus has provided the "way"!